Into the Dark

Suspense novel circa 1950
New Bedford, MA

By

Clement R. Beaulieu

Into the Dark

Suspense Novel Circa 1950 New Bedford, MA

By

Clement R. Beaulieu

Visit our website **at www.StillwaterPress.com** for more information.

First Stillwater River Publications Edition

ISBN-10: 0-9978778-4-7
ISBN-13: 978-0-9978778-4-7

1 2 3 4 5 6 7 8 9 10
Written by Clement R. Beaulieu
Front Cover Photo by Jo-Ann Beaulieu
Cover design by Dawn M. Porter.
Published by Stillwater River Publications, Glocester, RI, USA.

Into the Dark

To my sisters

Cozette and Joanne

The background of this fictional suspense story centers on the pre-teen years my sisters and I spent living in a triple decker in the north end of New Bedford. The time-line is circa 1950. The story is a creation of my imagination and any resemblance to actual persons or events is strictly coincidental.

A special thanks to my wife Jo-Ann who continues to support my writing, reading initial drafts and offering suggestions. For this novel she also provided the color photo used on the cover. She captured this scene of the setting sun looking out from our yard.

Again a special consideration goes to Lee Ann Bordas who critiqued and corrected the manuscript.

Into the Dark

Book One

Into the Dark

Book One

Chapter One

He's gone...

On a Saturday morning in Lent, Al and Janet Lepage's children were planning their day. Charlotte as usual had called them together in the front parlor. This was their work area that helped support Uncle Claude's fish and chip store.

Charlotte informed her younger siblings, "Mom told me last night that they had just about ran out of the newspapers they use to wrap the fish and the supply of bags used to carry the French fries is getting low. They won't have enough cut to size and stacked for the coming week."

Andrew, who was sitting crossed-leg on the floor perked up, saying "Today is a good day for collecting papers from the neighbors. Someone is usually at home on Saturday."

"You're right," agreed Charlotte.

"It's quite cold this morning," added Louise. "We'll have to dress warmly."

Charlotte looked sternly at her brother, and agreeing with her sister, emphasized, "We don't want any of your ranting that you're quite warm when you're pulling your wagon up and down the street. We can't have you catching one of your colds that keeps you out of school. Plus, this is getting to be one of the busiest times of the year for fish and chips. We need all hands on deck."

Andrew saluted his sister, "Yes, captain."

1

"As you know," continued Charlotte, "we are all driving up to Maine tomorrow to get a large supply of potatoes. Mom will be joining us. That's why she left earlier this morning with Dad to help Mémère today rather than tomorrow. And that's why she's asked us to help clean up the house before we get into our work for the restaurant."

Louise sat quietly on the nearby sofa. She knew that Charlotte had all these chores already well organized in her head. She awaited her assignment.

Charlotte started, "I'll clean the kitchen and pantry, do the dishes and wash the floor on my hands and knees." Charlotte added emphasis as she described the manner in which she would accomplish that task.

Louise quietly breathed a sigh of relief. She hated that job and knew it would never pass her older sister's inspection.

Charlotte pointed to Louise, "Mom asked that we wash down the sink and bath tub. We'll be using it tonight. You can do that. Mom said we didn't have to do the floor since it will be getting all wet. She'll clean it up after our baths. Louise, you can also dust the living room area and front parlor. Do a good job but don't take all day!"

Andrew knew he was next. Not so long ago, Charlotte would only ask him to stay out of the way while she and Louise did the chores. However, lately she was finding things that he could do around the house. She started, "I have three things I want you to do."

Andrew wide-eyed stared up to his sister. The list was getting longer each time. "First finish making your bed and remember no wrinkles in the sheets. I'll be pulling up the blanket when I inspect your work. Then tidy up your room. Everything off the floor."

Again Andrew saluted, "Yes, captain."

"While you're doing that, I'll gather the trash. You'll bring it downstairs and place it in the trash barrel. Remember to place the lid back on the barrel," directed Charlotte.

Andrew reflected on this with some amazement. He had always been rather clumsy and the flight of stairs to their third floor tenement was also a challenge.

Charlotte saw the concern in her brother's eyes. She added, "I've already looked at the amount of trash in the container under the kitchen sink. It's less than half full and not heavy. Just go slowly and hold on to the rail. You can do it."

This time Andrew didn't salute his sister. He felt a genuine pride in her selecting him to do this task.

"Lastly," Charlotte added. "I'll give you a wet rag and I want you to wipe down the baseboard in the parlor and living room. Keep out of Louise's way. When she dusts around the house she moves a lot of delicate things. I don't want you to bump into her and cause her to drop and break something."

"When we finish our chores," Charlotte continued, "we'll have some lunch. Mom left us some sandwich meat and bread. Then both of you will get dressed warmly and off you'll go to collect the newspapers. Stay on this side of the street. Go up as far as Mrs. Dupuis and not any closer to the Avenue. There is a lot of traffic there on a Saturday. In the meantime, I'll start cutting the bags for chips and stacking them together."

Into the Dark

Chapter Two

As they were finishing their lunch after completing their chores, Charlotte pointed to a basket holding apples that rested in the center of the dining room table. She announced, "Mom said we could each have one."

Andrew quickly snatched up a bright red one, "I'll bring it with me when we go out to fetch the newspapers."

"I'll eat mine when we get back," said Louise. "I don't like the taste and roughness of the peel in my mouth. As you know I take the time to peel it and remove the insides and cut the apple into strips. It's worth the trouble and work to just taste the juicy white of the apple." Both Charlotte and Andrew looked at her with a shrug of their shoulders. That was Louise being Louise.

Charlotte directed Andrew to take his heavy coat hanging on a hook in the back hallway. "And take your tuque," she insisted. Andrew just grunted.

As they reached the second floor landing Andrew and Louise looked at each other and breathed in a deep sigh. They were free from their older sister's instructions and anxious concerns about them.

When they reached the first floor entryway, they, as was their custom, quickly knocked and open the door to their grandmother's tenement. The room was quiet and empty but they heard some noise in the kitchen to their left. Mémère poked her head out and came to greet the two of them with big hugs.

"We're going to collect newspapers for Uncle Claude's restaurant," announced Andrew. "We're off."

Andrew retrieved his red wagon from the little shed in the back yard. Once he had rolled the wagon into the drive between the house, Louise closed the gate to the back yard. Andrew announced, "I'm too hot already and I haven't started pulling the wagon with newspapers in it."

He took off his tuque and placed it in his left coat pocket. His right pocket contained the red apple he had taken from the dining room table. "Let's get going," he proclaimed for all to hear.

As they reached the end of the driveway, Louise said, "Let's go up toward the Avenue first. We usually gather more papers along that longer route."

Andrew agreed, "We'll go all the way to Mrs. Dupuis' house first. Then we'll pick up papers along the way back. It will be easier for me to pull the wagon coming down the street." Louise helped in getting the papers from the neighbors but it was Andrew who stacked them in his wagon and pulled it along. Today was a bit windy so Andrew had picked up a fairly large stone next to the trash can. It was used exclusively to lay on the newspapers so that they wouldn't blow away. Andrew had informed everyone in the house about the use of the stone and said, "Make sure you don't get rid of it. It's just the right size. Keep it near the trash can." This collecting of newspapers was a serious business.

A few houses up the street, Mr. Lapierre was sweeping his front porch and stairs. He asked, "Are you collecting papers today?" Louise answered, "Yes. We just started." Mr. Lapierre told them, "I'll go through the house and bring the papers to the front porch." Andrew replied, "We'll pick them up on our way down."

A few tenement houses further up, Peter, Andrew's friend from school, was helping his dad wash the family car at the end of the driveway. Peter had a bucket of soapy water and with a big wet sponge and was spreading it all over the rear of their Chevrolet. Peter's father asked, "You collecting newspapers?" Louise again was the spokesperson, "We've just about run out of our supply."

Andrew had been distracted. He was envious of Peter who was getting quite wet but had the biggest smile on his face. "Peter," his father said, "go tell your sister to collect the papers and bring them outside. I'll rinse down the car with the hose while you're gone."

"We'll be back," said Andrew as he watched the soapy water being rinsed off the car and flowing down the driveway into the street next to the curb. Andrew loved Saturdays. It was day for doing different and fun things.

When they eventually reached Mrs. Dupuis's house the two of them walked to the rear of the house. It was Louise's job to knock on doors. Andrew waited near the bottom step near his wagon. Andrew remembered what his father had told him about why people on this side of the street used mostly their back entrance and those on the other side of the street used the front porch as their entrance. On this side of the street, the back entrance faced the south and the sun kept the wooden stairway from freezing and being slippery in the winter. On the other side of the street the front porch and stairs faced the sun.

Louise eventually came out and gave Andrew a collection of newspapers. "Mrs. Dupuis said that young Miss Michaud stores her papers in her hallway closet on the second floor. She's working today at the Acushnet Company but gave Mrs. Dupuis instructions that we could collect her papers whenever we came by. I'll go get them and bring them down."

"This is turning out to be a great collection day," said Andrew. Even before they reached Mr. Lapierre's house on their way down the street, the wagon was filled. The stone kept the papers from blowing away but Andrew announced, "We can't add much more or they'll fly away. Let's bring these home and come back for the rest."

After depositing the papers in the back hallway, the two of them continued their way up the street retrieving newspapers. Charlotte came down from the third floor and brought up each load and began slicing the newspaper sheets in half.

Into the Dark

Chapter Three

After their fourth trip up the street, Louise said, "Ok, let's go down the street toward the mills. There are only a few houses before we get to Belleville Avenue. It shouldn't take us too long." A series of mills were located across Belleville and stretched as far as the eye could see. Quite a few people in the neighborhood, including a couple of their aunts, worked in those mills.

The house just next to them was mostly occupied by relatives. One of Pépère's brothers owned that house. Their cousins, Paul and Brian, were playing marbles in their driveway. Andrew shouted out, "We are almost finished collecting papers. I'll come and join you. I have a brand new shooter."

Off they went. Next house over they picked up newspapers at two of the tenements. Andrew was carefully stacking them in the wagon, when a man in a heavy plaid jacket approached the two youngsters. "You looking to collect newspapers?" Louise said, "yes" and Andrew nodded. He began thinking we can finish this work in no time and I'll go play with the boys.

The man told them, "Follow me. It's just around the corner." Then he started out leading them down the street. Just before they reached the corner on Belleville Avenue, there was a large empty lot on the corner. It was full of bushes and weeds. Most adults called it an eyesore. In early Spring some neighbors would gather together and clean and tidy it up, but as the heat of summer came along the area was left to fend for itself. There was a fairly well used path that crossed through the lot.

The man started to enter the path and looked back saying, "Come, follow along. It's just around the next corner." Before entering the path Louise looked at Andrew, shaking her head and said, "Let's get out of here." She was beginning to get frightened. They had never ventured into this direction before. When they left their street, it was always in the other direction that took them the two blocks to St. Joseph's School.

Andrew started to pull the wagon into the pathway. Louise kept saying, "Turn around Andrew." Frightened, she now started running up the street toward the safety of their house. She thought she heard Andrew turn in his tracks, pulling his wagon to follow her up the street.

Louise didn't stop running until she reached their driveway. She bent over catching her breath and eventually looked back down the street expecting to see Andrew pulling his wagon homeward. There was no one on the sidewalk as far as her eyes could see. Her heart dropped. Then she thought, "Maybe he stopped next door and was talking with his cousins who were playing marbles." She went to see them but her cousins said, "We haven't seen him."

Louise couldn't say anything. She didn't dare to go any further down the street. She ran back to their house and burst into Mémère's first floor tenement. Mémère was straightening out the living room. When she saw the fright on Louise's face, she came over quickly and asked, "What's the matter Louise?"

Louise was still out of breath and tears were spilling down her face. Mémère knelt before her and said, "Go slowly. What's happened?"

Louise finally blurted out, "I've lost Andrew."

Still kneeling before her, Mémère said, "Tell me what happened."

Louise told her about going down the street, meeting a strange man who said he had some newspapers and how they had started following him, then she had become frightened when they reached the empty corner lot, and she had told Andrew not to follow the stranger into the path. "I told Andrew to run back home. I started running and thought he was right behind me. But when I looked down the street, he wasn't there."

"I'll go with you and look for him," said her Mémère. "First, let me wake up Joseph. He worked the overnight shift. I'll have him help us look for Andrew."

As they were in the rear hallway, Louise asked her Mémère, "Should I go upstairs and tell Charlotte? She'll be angry with me for not watching over Andrew.

"Yes, go tell her," answered Mémère, "but tell her to stay put and that your uncle Joseph and I will be looking for him. I'm sure we'll find him."

When Louise came running back down the stairway, her uncle Joseph who had put on his work pants and heavy jacket joined them. His shoes were still untied but he said to Louise, "Let's go. Show me where you guys went."

Mémère still had her flowery apron peeking out from the mid-length coat she had thrown over her shoulders. As they started down the street the group stopped in the neighbor's driveway where the two boys were still playing their game. Mémère asked, "Have you seen Andrew?" "No," both boys answered simultaneously. "Is something the matter," asked Paul. The boys stopped playing their game and came to the sidewalk.

"Just stay here," advised Joseph. "We're going down the street to look for him."

Mémère held Louise's trembling hand tightly in her warm hands. The three of them walked steadily down the street looking into the driveways that lay between the three deckers. In one of the driveways a neighbor's car was parked at the end. Joseph said, "Wait for me here. I'll go see if Andrew might be hiding in front of the car."

In a flash he was back. "Not there, and the gate to the back yard is closed. The yard was empty."

In a few minutes they were at the unkempt lot that had unnerved Louise. "I'll run down the path to Belleville Avenue. Maybe I'll see them walking to the corner of the next street or around that corner. I'll be right back."

Mémère held Louise close to her. As she was being held, Louise closed her eyes and prayed so hard that Andrew would be found just around the corner. She felt so badly. Her brother, who was just a little more than a year younger than she, was her constant companion. The way their birthdays had fallen and the fact that the year when Andrew had started school there was a bumper crop of kindergarten children, Andrew had skipped kindergarten and joined Louise in the same classroom of the first grade. She had been unofficially chosen to be his protector and guardian. She had always taken that responsibility very seriously.

Into the Dark

Chapter Four

Joseph ran the length of the rough pathway that crossed diagonally through the messy lot. Once he almost fell as one of his shoe strings got caught on some briars that lined the path. When he quickly reached Belleville, he looked both ways but didn't see Andrew or his wagon. He raced to the corner at his right and looked up the street but again no one was immediately in sight. He ran up the street a ways looking into driveways and yards. Nothing.

When he started back down the street, he noticed a man standing on the opposite corner who was smoking a cigarette. He crossed over to him and asked, "Did you see a little boys pulling a red wagon?"

"No," he answered. "I just got here. A friend is picking me up in a few minutes. We're going to a bar for drinks and a game of cards. After all, it is Saturday."

Joseph decided that he had to return to his mother and Louise even though he hadn't anything to help quiet their fear. Rather than taking the pathway across the lot, he decided to go to the corner and come back up their street. As he ran back, he looked quickly into the brushes of the lot and across the Avenue to the sidewalk adjacent to the mills that lined that side of the street. At the corner there was an opening between two mills that gave a view of the Acushnet River. It was glistening in the afternoon sun. Silently, he prayed, "Please God, he didn't go in that direction."

A few seconds later he reached his mother and niece, Louise. Joseph looked into his mother's eyes. No words were spoken between them except for the volumes of feelings and fear each shared with the other. Both didn't want to upset Louise.

Mémère looked at Louise, "Let's go back to the house. Your sister Charlotte is waiting for us and will be wondering what is happening."

She turned to her youngest son Joseph and instructed him, "When we get to the house call Janet. She's at her mother's house helping her. Tell her what's happening. Al is supposed to pick her up later this afternoon. She told me she had planned to be home in time to make supper for her family. That's probably about an hour from now."

As they walked back together, Joseph added to the plan, "I'm not sure where Al is right now on his route. However, he usually stops at Labonte's pharmacy just before he comes back home. I'll call the pharmacy and tell Ben to alert Al."

When they reached the house Mémère took off her coat and hung it in the hall closet. She gazed at Louise and said, "Let's get a couple of lemons from my fridge and we'll go upstairs to make some lemonade with your sister."

Louise was opening the door of their tenement and calling out to Charlotte. Mémère was still ten or more steps behind her and breathing heavily.

By the time Mémère had entered through the doorway, Charlotte had come racing from the front parlor where she was working on the restaurant projects. While she worked she had become quite anxious about the turn of events.

"What's happening?" Looking behind Mémère she stammered, "Didn't you find Andrew?"

Mémère answered quietly trying to calm the highly excitable Charlotte, "Your uncle Joseph will continue to look for him. He can't be far away. He's calling your mother at your other Mémère's. Your father will be picking her up soon and they'll be back with us in no time. Your father will probably know exactly some of Andrew's favorite hiding places. In the meantime, help me make some lemonade. I'm thirsty with all this running around."

Louise was just standing there almost paralyzed with fear she wondered when Charlotte would start to question her and blame her. Instead Charlotte came over to her sister and hugged her, saying, "Give me your coat and hat and I'll hang it up in the hall." Charlotte had a sudden innate sense that her sister was frightened to death and didn't need any additional badgering from her.

When she came back into the room, Charlotte grabbed her sister's hand and led her to the kitchen where Mémère was cutting the two lemon in half. She asked, "Where does your mother keep the lemon squeezer?" as she looked through the kitchen drawers. "Oh, here it is."

"And where does she keep her supply of sugar?" Mémère questioned.

Charlotte pointed to the open shelf to the left of the stove.

Mémère instructed Louise, "Now Louise get me a tray of ice cubes from your mother's new fridge."

Mémère wanted to keep the girls' minds busy and distracted from frightful thoughts. However, her own mind was racing all over the place. The Lindbergh kidnapping that had happened about twenty years earlier was still a hot topic of conversation. It was a fear that entered every woman's heart as she looked out for her children.

Downstairs Joseph had called and informed his sister-in-law, Janet. He tried to keep his words calm, trying to indicate the situation could be resolved by the time she returned home with Al. He continued, "Ma is with your two girls' upstairs."

Joseph next called Ben the druggist. Ben told him, "Al just left here on his way to pick up Janet." When Joseph related what was happening just down the street, he told him, "Officer Matt Cyr is with me in the back room of the pharmacy." After a brief pause, Ben continued, "Matt said he'll be right down there. He'll meet you at the front of the house. He said for you to try to find some neighbors who will help with the search."

Into the Dark

Book Two

Into the Dark

Book Two

Chapter Five

Terrified...

Officer Matthew Cyr came running down the street. He carried a weapon on his side. It bounced off his pretty hefty thighs. He had just finished his shift but was ready to offer assistance. He had informed Ben to call his Captain at the precinct and as he left the back room of the pharmacy, he also asked Ben, "Oh, yes. Will you call my wife and tell her I may be late for dinner?"

Joseph Lepage, who was standing close to the front of his home awaiting the policeman, was only able to recruit one member for the search group. Next door his Uncle Peter had heard about all the commotions from his sons and out of curiosity came out to talk to Joseph. The usual adults who hung around the neighborhood on a Saturday were out and about.

Joseph went out to meet Officer Cyr as he approached the house.

"Joe, what's going on?" asked the Officer.

"Matt," answered Joseph, "my nephew is missing."

Joseph and Matthew had both attended St. Joseph' School together. Joseph was about five years younger and had been in class with Matthew's sister. They knew each other.

Joe started telling Matt of his initial search. Uncle Peter was standing nearby getting the first account of the situation. He immediately looked concerned, and asked the Officer, "Are there any predators around?"

Matthew Cyr informed him, "the police are always on the lookout for anyone that might prey on children. However, I'm not aware of any serious concern in this neighborhood."

As they were beginning to strategize, Al and Janet Lepage came driving into the driveway in his old grey panel truck.

Both came to the sidewalk looking for information. Janet quickly assumed that nothing had changed and excused herself, "I'm going up to see the children."

Officer Cyr said, "More support will be coming shortly from the precinct." He looked at Al and questioned, "How old is your son?" Al answered, "He just turned nine."

The Officer continued, "Can you get a recent photo of him?" Al nodded.

"We will organize a search party. It's getting close to four o'clock. We have about another two hours before it starts getting **dark**."

All of a sudden two police cars came down the street. The red lights on the vehicle were on but the sirens were silent. Three new policemen joined the group.

Al looked pleadingly at his brother Joseph, "Is this really happening?"

After being briefed, Sergeant Walter Demanche took control of the situation and started to strategize the search for young Andrew. He pointed to the team of one of the squad cars, "You'll go with Joseph and search the empty lot and the neighboring street around the corner. Look high and low. You know this neighborhood. Keep an eye out for anything that looks odd or out of the ordinary."

Sergeant Demanche turned his attention to Al Lepage and said, "I know this must be horrifying for you. An inspector from downtown will be here shortly. Go get that photo of Andrew and try to reassure everyone in the family that we are doing all we can."

As Al returned with the photo, an unmarked police car arrived at their address. Al was introduced to Inspector Daniel O'Malley. They both instantly recognized each other. A few years back their paths had crossed.

The Inspector listened attentively to the narrative the Sergeant was relating to him. Al was constantly learning new things about the disappearance of his son.

Al interrupted, "You're saying that my daughter Louise claimed that a man enticed them to follow him beyond their normal boundaries?" When Sergeant nodded, Al turned to the Inspector, "Have there been any such situations happening around here?

Inspector O'Malley had learned early in his career not to bluff or hide information from victims. He answered, "There have been a few incidents in other parts of the city but not around here." O'Malley knew that this information would not be especially consoling to a father whose son was missing.

Inspector O'Malley was looking at the photo of young Andrew when the squad car that had gone down the street returned. One of the officers took Andrew's red wagon out of the trunk. "We found this in the corner lot. It was hidden in the bushes."

Joseph came up to his brother, Al. They held on to each other. The worst of what could be expected had been realized. Andrew was not lost but had been kidnapped.

Into the Dark

Chapter Six

Inspector O'Malley was suddenly facing a very different development in the case of the missing Andrew. Time was of the essence. It would be getting **dark** soon and further searching would quickly become more difficult.

He turned to Al Lepage, Andrew's father, "Are there any secret places where your son Andrew likes to hide? Does he play hide and seek with his friends?"

Al answered, "Yes. They usually play in our back yard but also in other yards in the neighborhood where his friends live. Mostly nearby."

"OK, go with your brother and these two Officers and do a thorough search," instructed the Inspector.

O'Malley instructed Sergeant Demanche to accompany Andrew's uncle Peter to visit the neighbors.

In the meantime, O'Malley conferred with Officer Matt Cyr who had been the first on the scene. "We need a good description of the man who was directing the children to follow him."

"From all I know so far, Louise was the only one other than Andrew who saw him," answered Officer Cyr.

O'Malley instructed the Officer, "Go across the street and knock on doors. See if anyone might have observed any of this happening. Someone may have been looking out a window or sitting on the front porch."

A few minutes later Sergeant Demanche and Uncle Peter came back from their search. Some of the neighbors who were home had assisted them. They had come up empty. Sergeant Demanche stated, "None of the neighbors observed anything during the time in question. Most of the living areas in these houses face toward the back, so no one was looking out toward the street. Most of the women in the tenements were busy in their kitchen, and some of the older people in the house don't normally sit in the front parlors. That room is kept for special occasions."

Another car approached the house. A young woman evidently dressed in the white outfit of nurse looked inquiringly at the police cars in front the house and the gathering on the sidewalk. She drove into the driveway.

Nurse Martha Lepage quickly exited her vehicle and leaving the car door ajar, came rushing to the group on the sidewalk. "Is something wrong?" she asked directing her question to the man in the police uniform. She quickly turned her attention to the gentleman in the long trench coat. He gave the bearing of being in charge. "I live here. I just finished my shift at St. Luke's Hospital."

Inspector O'Malley acknowledged her and gently related a brief account of Andrew's disappearance. Martha looked crushed. Suddenly Martha realized that she had met the Inspector on a previous occasion. Some months earlier she had met with him in reference to Lieutenant Mortimer Weigand. It was only recently that her brother, Claude, had told her the weird story of the Lieutenant's disappearance.

O'Malley quickly realized that he had just received an unexpected resource in Nurse Lepage. He had previously learned that she had been a psych nurse while serving on the West Coast in a Naval Hospital. He needed to get a description from the young Louise without further frightening her.

O'Malley asked Martha, "Will you assist me in interviewing Louise? I'm assuming she's your niece. We need to be tender with her. I haven't met her yet, but I suspect it's been quite traumatic for her. We need a report of what happened and as accurate a description of the man in question. I think she would trust you."

Martha readily agreed.

Inspector O'Malley instructed Sergeant Demanche to keep watch from the sidewalk. Looking to Martha, he asked, "Do you think we could question Louise inside the house?"

Martha nodded and rushed to the car to grab her purse firmly closing and locking the car door. Suddenly security had become a concern in her very familiar and comfortable neighborhood.

The back door of the tenement house opened without the use of a key. Only in the late evening hours, after everyone was thought to be in, did the last person might think to lock the outside door that led to the hallway and stairs to the other two tenements.

Martha called out but no one was in the apartment. O'Malley ventured, "I believe your mother is still upstairs with your nieces and their mother who just returned home a short time ago. Do you think you could ask Louise to join us here accompanied by her mother? I think it would be best to interview Louise without her sister. Also it occurs to me that your own mother may be an equally supportive companion for Louise. Your mother did participate in the original search for Andrew. You make the call."

As Martha rushed out of the apartment, O'Malley stepped out into the rear hallway. It was his professional choice to always have a person with him when he was in someone's private space and property. He offered this advice to young recruits when he participated in their training.

A few minutes later Martha was leading a very frightened Louise and her mother to the first floor apartment. O'Malley observed a petrified young girl. Her eyes were deep set and the area around them was red. She was rubbing away tears as she entered the room. Her mother stood behind her and supported her with caressing hands on her young daughter's shoulders.

O'Malley had made a quick observation of the living room. He invited Louise and her mother to sit on a large comfortable and well-used couch. Louise chose the section closest to the left stuffed arm of the couch. Janet sat beside her. Louise settled in deeply. She was like in a safe cocoon.

O'Malley set up two living room chairs across from the couch. Martha's chair was placed just a bit closer than the Inspector's chair. Without guidance or instruction, Martha started, "Louise, this is Inspector O'Malley and he is helping us in looking for your brother."

Louise's eyes had been turned down but O'Malley noticed that she sneaked a peak toward him. "That's a good sign," he reflected.

"Can you tell us what happened to you and your brother earlier today?" asked Martha. Louise looked at her aunt. Except for crying, Louise had not spoken a word since entering the house with her mémère. Martha reached out and touched Louise's right hand which she had just returned to her lap after another brush to her eyes. The other hand was out of sight, tucked into the side of the soft arm of the couch. Janet held her closely and without saying anything was giving signals of encouragement.

In a cracked and strained voice, Louise related, "We were just about finishing collecting newspapers..." Louise stopped. She hardly recognized her own voice.

"And…," encouraged Martha.

"A man was suddenly by our side and he offered to give us some newspapers. He asked us to follow him," continued Louise.

Martha asked, "Did you see where he came from? Did he come up from behind you?"

"No," answered Louise. "I had just looked back to see Andrew pulling his wagon and following me."

"When you turned around was this man in front of you or on your side?" asked Martha.

Louise remembered, "He was right there on my left side. He seemed to come out of nowhere. He was just there."

Inspector O'Malley reflected, "This psych nurse is a real pro." She was leading the investigation with great delicacy but uncovering some important facts.

Aunt Martha continued, "So Louise the man appeared from the street side and not from the houses on your right?"

"That's right," answered Louise.

"Were there any cars or trucks parked along the side of the road?" asked Martha.

"There could have been but I didn't notice," and suddenly a flood of tears come down Louise's face. "Andrew would have noticed. He knew every car and make…" Janet's eyes also swelled with tears but she remained silent, holding her sensitive little Louise close to her.

Martha waited a while and eventually asked, "What did the man look like? What was he wearing?

Louise finally replied, "He was much taller than me and standing close to me. So I had to look up to see him. His face was round."

After a brief moment Louise continued, "He was wearing a coat similar to the one Uncle Pierre used when he went to Church."

Janet asked, "You mean the one with stripes and different colors?"

"Yes, that's the one," answered Louise.

Looking over briefly to the Inspector, Martha continued, "Was it the same colors as the plaid coat Uncle Pierre wore?"

"No," answered Louise rather quickly. "Uncle Pierre's coat had lots of red and orange. This one had darker colors gray and blue."

Martha took one last stab at getting a description of the stranger. "Did you noticed anything else about him as he walked in front of you and Andrew? Did he have a hat on? What was the color of his pants?"

Louise thought a while as she tried to recall the scene of the man walking ahead of them. She answered, "He wasn't wearing a hat. He was bald like Pépère with some dark hair near his ears."

Inspector O'Malley instinctively started to reach for his trusty notepad he always kept in the inner pocket of his suit coat, but held back as he thought such formality could possibly unnerve the young girl. There were a lot of precious details being revealed in the case. He decided he would later confer with nurse Martha about the accuracy of his notes. Together, he felt assured that they would recall the description of the man.

As O'Malley was having these reflections, Louise started up again, "The color of the pants was dark green or maybe dark brown.

The pants were not the type my father or uncles wear for work. I know, they were the kind of pants they wear for church on Sunday."

Louise gave both hands to Martha who held them on the girl's lap. "You've been doing a great job, Louise. This is very helpful information for the Inspector"

O'Malley smiled and nodded his head adding, "You're a brave girl."

Martha continued, "Can I ask you one last question?" Louise nodded and looked a little pensive. She sensed from Martha's manner that it may be a difficult one."

"When the man encouraged you and Andrew to follow him into the empty lot, did he turn around and look at you?" asked Martha.

"Yes," answered Louise rather quickly.

Martha asked, "What do you remember about his face? What did he look like?" All the adults present appreciated that this was the moment that Louise had become frightened and urged Andrew to turn around and run with her back to their home.

Louise closed her eyes. She didn't want to remember the scene. The man looked annoyed and angry. He reminded Louise of one of her teachers in her black habit who often enough would express impatience with some of the boys in class when they acted out. That had always terrified Louise.

"He was angry with me for slowing down," answered Louise. "He took off his glasses and waved them at us saying, 'Come on. It's just around the corner.' When he turned around, I nudged Andrew to start running back home with me."

Both Janet and Martha were consoling Louise, holding her securely in their embrace. Under her breath, they heard Louise say,

"I thought he was following me…" and tears flooded down her cheeks.

Inspector O'Malley touched Martha's shoulder and agreed with his gesture that it was time to comfort her niece.

"Thank you, Louise. I know that this remembering was very scary for you. You have been very brave."

Into the Dark

Chapter Seven

While Louise and her mother Janet were downstairs with the Police Inspector, Mémère suggested to Charlotte, "Let's make some supper for everyone. With everything going on, no one has eaten. Let's look around the kitchen."

When Mémère opened the refrigerator, she found some ground beef. Thinking a bit, she asked Charlotte, "Does your mother have any elbow macaroni?" Charlotte looked into the pantry and brought out a new package of Muellers. "Here's a box," said Charlotte. Looking further together, Mémère took out two large cans of stewed tomatoes and a smaller can of tomato paste. Looking at Charlotte, she exclaimed, "I think we have found all the ingredients to make a meal of American Chop Suey that will feed everyone." Mémère filled a large pot of water and placed it on the dining room oven/stove that also served as the source of heat for the apartment.

"Now, Charlotte," asked Mémère, "where does your mother keep her can opener?" Charlotte pointed to a top drawer to Mémère's left. "And here is the garlic press," Mémère added with a smile. "I just saw a garlic clove in your mother's fridge." Soon they were frying the ground beef in a large frying pan. Mémère had started with a little olive oil in the pan. Looking into Janet's spice cabinet, Mémère removed a bottle of oregano and bay leaves. "Now all we need is Worcestershire Sauce, she stated. Putting her finger up to her lips, she whispered to Charlotte, "That's my secret ingredient." Sure enough, Mémère found an opened bottle of Lea & Perrins Worcestershire Sauce in Janet's refrigerator.

Before long the water for the elbow macaroni was boiling. Mémère also added a small amount of olive oil to the water and encouraged Charlotte to empty the box of macaroni into it. "Just go slowly," cautioned Mémère, "it boils up a bit. Then stir it around so that the elbows don't stick together."

Both Mémère and Charlotte were moving away from the dismal thoughts and feelings that had recently overwhelmed them. Mémère reflected, "It was good to keep busy."

Soon the large pot was filled with a delicious meal of American Chop Suey.

When Louise and Janet returned to the third floor tenement, the smell of the popular comfort food welcomed them.

After some hugs, Mémère pointed to a large bowl, "I'll bring some downstairs for us to eat. There should be plenty for all of us as she pointed to the large pot standing to the side of the dining room stove, keeping the meal warm.

In the meantime, Sergeant Demanche suggested to Al Lepage, "I think that your family could use your support right now. Go join them. We will continue our search out here." For now, the Sergeant thought it best not to expose Andrew's father to any more of this investigation. So with shoulders bent over, Al walked slowly to the back entrance.

Mémère met Al coming up the stairway. Her son looked so distraught. Her oldest son who always smiled and was full of energy looked beaten. She said as she kissed him on the cheek, "Go to your girls. They need you, and you need them."

Louise looked up as her father entered the apartment and hastily asked, "Did you find Andrew?"

Seeing the woeful expression on his face, Louise started to cry. Her sister Charlotte came up to her and held her tightly.

"Why didn't I grab him by the hand and pull him to follow me?" she sobbed.

"I was only thinking of myself. I'm such a scaredy cat," Louise added.

Janet tried to comfort her, "It's very important that you are safe. Let's not give up on Andrew."

Al added, "He's become quite grown up. Doesn't he surprise all of us by what he comes up with? As your mother says, let's keep our hopes up."

Janet called them to the dining room table, "Come let's eat this fine meal that Mémère and Charlotte made for us. After we finish your father will wash the dishes and I'll help you with your baths. It's getting late."

Although, everyone was upset, they ate heartily, including Louise. It was one of the family's favorite dish. Their stomachs were churning with anxiety and fear, but all were famished and the smooth, tasty noodles slipped easily down their throats.

Charlotte as was the custom in the household took her bath first. She was the eldest of the children. When she was finished, Janet added some additional hot water from the large kettle on the dining room stove so that the water would be warm enough for Louise. Without saying it, the two girls remembered how they insisted that Andrew always had to be the last of the children to take a bath. He was always dirtier than his sisters and would leave a mess in the water. Today they were ready to give him the preferred spot in the rotation.

Into the Dark

Chapter Eight

After interviewing Louise, Inspector O'Malley had quietly excused himself and rejoined the group of men gathering on the sidewalk. Long shadows were being cast by the houses and the few trees of the neighborhood. O'Malley turned up the collar of his trench coat. The evening was getting colder and it was quite a contrast from the warmth indoors.

It was evident that Andrew had not been located. Officer Matt Cyr was just coming across the street from combing that side of the neighborhood. He started to tell of his findings, "I concentrated on the homes at the lower part of the street. I knocked on the front doors, and without trying to frighten the residents who answered their doors, asked whether they had seen a young boy or anything out of the ordinary, a stranger, an unfamiliar vehicle in the neighborhood this afternoon."

O'Malley could sense that the Officer had discovered something.

The Officer related, "One woman who lives in the second house from the corner had enjoyed the late afternoon sun on her first floor porch earlier in the day. She thought she observed some activity in the empty lot but hadn't paid too much attention. Plus, her view was somewhat obstructed by a **dark** green van parked on that side of the street. When asked if she had seen that vehicle before, she answered, 'The people across the street don't have a van. I think I've seen a van further up the street when I walk up to the Labonte's pharmacy.' She was the only one who had something to say about the incident. Everyone else was at home and doing their normal Saturday afternoon chores."

Office Matt Cyr continued, "The only other thing that I discovered was that one of Andrew's uncles lives across the street." And pointing to the white six family house, "He lives there with his wife and in-laws." His mother-in-law was the only one at home and was stunned to learn that young Andrew was missing. She was going immediately to call her daughter and inform her of the situation. Looking at his notes, Officer Cyr added, "Mrs. Saulnier told me that her daughter and husband wouldn't be able to get home until after nine o'clock. They run the fish and chip shop. That's why the young Lepage children were gathering newspapers."

Joseph Lepage who was still among those gathered on the sidewalk, affirmed, "Yes, my brother Al's kids have been collecting newspapers for the restaurant ever since it opened over a year ago."

Inspector O'Malley looked about and observed, "It's going to be **dark** soon. Joseph, could you ask what Andrew was wearing when he went out this afternoon. Come back quickly."

Officer Cyr commented, "I know many of these Lepages. They are a large family. They will be devastated if Andrew isn't found soon."

A few minutes later Joseph Lepage returned and excitedly told the Inspector, "Andrew was wearing his pea coat that his mother had made for him that resembled the one his uncle Claude had worn while in the Navy. He had also taken his green tuque with him."

The Inspector asked Joseph, "If it's okay with you, I would like you to return with these two policemen to the empty lot and scour it for anything that may have belonged to Andrew."

One of the policeman took charge of the search. He instructed them, "We'll walk side by side from this side to the end of the lot and come back here again. We'll follow that grid so as not to miss any area." He removed some bags from the back seat of the squad car and instructed, "Pick up anything along the way of your search except for any rotting garbage. We are looking for anything that Andrew may have left behind as well as the man in question."

The **dark** shadows from the three decker to the west of the lot were making it increasingly difficult to see into the thick brush and tall weeds. The search was hampered by the necessity of avoiding the dog poop that covered much of the area. It took the searchers about twenty minutes to complete their task.

Under a streetlight at the corner of Belleville Avenue, Joseph looked quickly through the items gathered by the two policeman and indicated, "I don't recognize anything that might have belonged to Andrew." Most of the stuff was litter, soda and beer bottles, parts of a broken tea cup, papers and rags, an old shoe – certainly, not the pea coat or tuque that Andrew had worn earlier in the day."

When they returned, Inspector O'Malley informed them that the search would have to resume in the morning. Front porch lights were coming on throughout this section of the neighborhood. People were gathered looking out with curiosity and one could hear the muffled chatter of conversation surrounding them.

Into the Dark

Chapter Nine

Inspector Daniel O'Malley informed those gathered on the sidewalk that he was returning to the central police station. Slowly the few men of the neighborhood who had joined the group went back to their residences, including Joseph. Joseph was evidently distraught and continued shaking his head in disbelief.

The Inspector informed the policemen who had joined him that he would be in touch with their precinct captain, "I'll be suggesting that there be a regular police presence in the neighborhood overnight. It will bring some reassurance to the residents who have been frightened by this incident."

"One last thing," continued O'Malley. "Inform your precinct captain that I have a pretty good description of this stranger. I'll get someone to put together a composite picture and we'll distribute the picture to the precincts. We'll also search our files for any known deviant and see if we find a match."

Joseph entered the first floor apartment to find his mother and Martha sitting at the table having a cup of tea. A large bowl of American Chop Suey and a loaf of Sunbeam bread remained at the center of the table. His mother offered him something to eat but he refused and said, "I'm having myself a beer." He took a bottle of Pickwick Ale, his father's favorite, from the refrigerator.

Martha told him that Louise had been a real trooper in relating the frightening episode for the Inspector. "But I know that she is carrying a profound sense of guilt. This will not be easy for her. Andrew and she have always been so close," added Martha.

"I told Janet I would go back upstairs later. I thought it would be best for Al and Janet to have their own private time together with Louise and Charlotte."

"I called your father," Joseph's mother informed him. "Tonight is a late night at the social club but the other bartender readily offered to close up the place once the group begins to thin out. Your father couldn't say much with all the noise in the background. He will be home as soon as possible."

"When I called Claude at the restaurant," added Martha, "he told me that Anne's mother had already called them. They were very busy but should be getting home soon after nine with our sister, Clara, who is helping them today. They'll put off the big weekend clean up until tomorrow."

"I wish I could do something," stated a fidgety Joseph. He abruptly stood up from the table, "This sitting around doing nothing is driving me crazy."

Mémère agreed and said, "I don't want to even think of what Andrew may be going though. It's just too awful."

Martha was eager to go upstairs to aid Louise, but from her training she also recognized that she was needed here. "Maybe we could pray," she offered.

Her mother promptly responded to the suggestion by asking, "Will you say the rosary with me?" After clearing the table, she lit a candle before the statue of the Virgin Mary, took out her beads and kneeling before the statue began the rosary in her accustomed and familiar French language.

Both Martha and Joseph hadn't said the rosary in French for a long time, Martha even more so. But the rhythm of the words became increasingly familiar. Martha knelt by the side of her mother and eventually Joseph knelt down behind them using the chair as a prie-dieu.

The repetitious words brought some calmness to the group. Joseph however continued to try to come up with some plan of action, wondering, "What could he do? Where could he go?"

Soon after saying the rosary, they heard someone in the rear hallway. Joseph rushed to the door and on opening it saw that his father had arrived. His mother came to him and began to sob as he held her. She had been holding back her tears for the sake of the others. In the safety of his arms she freely shared her grief.

They sat around the table. Pépère was trying to catch up with the terrible events of the day. Martha made some more tea for herself and her mother. Joseph offered his father a Pickwick. He readily agreed, "I didn't take time to have my regular night cap before leaving the social club." Once the bottle cap was removed, he took a long slug and setting it down on the table breathed in deeply.

Eventually, Martha excused herself, "I'm going upstairs to see how they're doing and see if I can be of help."

Aunt Martha found her nieces sitting side by side on the living room couch in their pajamas and bathrobes. She sat beside them. Janet was tidying up the apartment.

Aunt Martha commented on the look of the girls' hair and the aroma of the soap they had used in their bath. Both girls however were quiet. Deep in their own gloomy thoughts. It was a striking contrast from the exciting chatter that always met her when she joined the girls.

After a while Janet asked, "Martha, will you help the girls get to bed? We are all tired."

The girls shared a room that had two twin beds. Charlotte asked Louise, "Do you want to share my bed with me?"

Louise replied, "Maybe, for a little while. I don't know if I can sleep thinking of Andrew still out there."

Martha tucked the two girls into Charlotte's bed. She sat on Louise's bed and said, "I'll lay down here for a while. I'm exhausted."

Before long Martha could hear the steady breathing of her nieces. They had fallen asleep. Martha quietly tiptoed out of the bedroom.

Janet and Martha sat on the couch together. Al had gone downstairs.

Slowly Janet let down her defenses and shared the distress and terror that was beneath the surface of her outward composure. Again Martha suggested that they might pray together.

Sitting together on the couch the two women prayed the rosary. This time it was in English. Janet remembered how she had adapted the rosary she said with her children during the Friday evenings of Lent. Andrew had always been such a fidget and couldn't last the entire praying of the rosary. She had given him an old set of beads to keep his hands busy and instead of saying the entire prayer to Mary, they would simply repeat the first two words – Hail Mary, Hail Mary... Andrew could handle that and the girls didn't complain either.

Into the Dark

Book Three

Into the Dark

Book Three

Chapter Ten

Concerted efforts…

Anne Lepage was closing up the fish and chip store. She had placed the 'CLOSED' sign in the window of the front door and pulled the shade down. Her sister-in-law, Clara, was wiping down the tables and setting aside the salt shakers and vinegar dispensers. Usually they would fill these up ready for the following week but today they were in a rush to get home.

Anne collected the bills and coins from the cash drawer and placed them into a light brown cloth bag that tied up at the top. The name 'Merchants Bank' was printed on the side. Anne's mother would count up the receipts for the day and prepare a deposit.

Clara cleaned the area behind the counter. She placed the remaining coleslaw into a covered container so she could bring it home to the family. Since the restaurant didn't open again until Wednesday a fresh batch of Claude's recipe would be made. This Lenten season Claude had introduced this new item to the menu. From his days as a cook in the Navy Seabees, Claude had perfected a sugar/vinegar cole slaw that had become very popular with their clientele. Along with the shredded cabbage, he used a small amount of shredded carrots and diced green peppers. He added a dash of celery seed and mustard seed and salt to taste. For the few that preferred mayonnaise, he made a smaller batch without the sugar and vinegar.

Claude had added this item to the menu to help bring in some additional revenue. He had finally revealed to his wife Anne his gambling habit that had led him to take money from their savings. The couple was still working through this deception.

Both women could hear Mrs. Cora Mayfield and Claude cleaning up the area behind a swinging door where the fish and chips were cooked in the friolators. Mrs. Mayfield was always very tired by Saturday night. On Wednesday and Thursday, she had filleted many pounds of fresh haddock and had spent long hours beside Claude frying the fish on Fridays and Saturdays. Claude told her about the disappearance of his nephew and said, "We will be closing as quickly as possible after the last customer. Members of the Lepage clan will gather Sunday or early in the week to give the place a thorough cleaning."

Cora gratefully responded, "I don't mind an earlier departure. I think my age is catching up with me. But I'm worried about your little nephew. Have you heard anymore?"

"No," answered Claude. "That's why we're going home as soon as we can to see what's been happening and to see if there is any way we can help."

Before 9 o'clock Mrs. Mayfield had taken her bus to the south end of the city. Anne, Clara and Claude were on the bus going in the opposite direction.

Anne held Claude's hand on her lap. He could sense her warm support at a possible unexpected tragedy for the family. The rather cool reception and feeling that existed between them since his revelation seemed to be lifting. He appreciated that but couldn't excuse or lift the heavy weight of guilt that stayed with him. Momentarily distracted from the concern for his nephew Andrew, Claude recalled the moment at the police station that had unraveled his hidden life.

Into the Dark

Chapter Eleven

A few months before Andrew's abduction, Claude had revealed to the police the elaborate scheme that his employer, Lieutenant Mortimer Weigand, had designed that had enabled him to disappear.

Claude Lepage remembered how he had sat across from Inspector O'Malley in the small interview room. He was totally exhausted. The dark secret he had kept to himself for almost a year had been revealed. In one sense he felt liberated. The hold that his past employer, Mortimer Weigand, had over him had been released.

Detective Joseph Barrett, who had remained standing during the entire interview was also fatigued and completely drained. He had started to wheeze and cough. Inspector O'Malley had offered him the well-ironed handkerchief that his wife, Maria, placed in his lapel pocket of his business suits each morning.

Joe had nodded and accepted the handkerchief. He covered his mouth and spit up the thick phlegm that had choked off his breathing. The Inspector advised Joe, "Go outside for a breath of fresh air. I'll finish up here. You did a great job. Ask Mrs. Glavin to come to the interview room with her steno pad."

Claude recalled how the tenacious Detective Barrett kept putting him on his heels. Every time Claude seemed to recover in supporting his original story of discovering Mr. Weigand hanging from the rafters of his office, Joe had brought up a detail that he had uncovered in his investigation that undermined Claude's statements.

Once Detective Barrett left the room, Inspector O'Malley had turned his attention to Claude. He recollected the Inspector's words, "Thank you for revealing to us the facts surrounding the disappearance of Lieutenant Mortimer Weigand. Mrs. Glavin, our secretary, will be joining us and will take down a statement of our examination of the case and the information you have provided. Once she has typed out your statement and you have signed it, you will be free to go."

Claude had sat quietly across the table from the Inspector. A great burden had been lifted from his shoulders. However, it had also evoked a pervasive sense of guilt. He could hear the words of his brother, Al, who had advised him to share with his wife, Anne, the web of his gambling and lies that had precipitated the intrigue with Mr. Weigand. Again he had promised himself that he would tell Anne. He felt so ashamed and knew that his guileless and innocent wife hadn't deserved to be treated so dreadfully by him.

Claude recalled the secretary who took down his statement. She was a rather heavy set middle aged women dressed in a black skirt and white blouse with a ruffled type collar and front. Her hair was pinned up in a bun similar to how one of Claude's sisters wore her long brown hair. However, Mrs. Glavin's hair was turning gray. Claude had been raised in a household with mostly older sisters and remembered how he had felt quite comfortable in her presence.

The Inspector had explained, "Claude, I want you to relate to Mrs. Glavin the particulars and elements that led to Mr. Weigand's disappearance. She will be writing your words in short-hand. Occasionally, she or I may interrupt your account for the sake of clarity. However, it is most important that this is your statement in your own words and relates to the incident as truthfully and accurately as you remember. This is a statement that may be used in a court of law. Any part of your statement that could be proven to be a lie could lead to charges. This is a serious matter."

Earlier in the interview, Claude had sensed a certain support and understanding from the Inspector. Detective Joe Barrett had been like a bloodhound. Now that the Detective had left the room, Inspector O'Malley became the inquisitor. As Claude related his account to Mrs. Glavin, O'Malley had kept glancing at his notes.

Inspector O'Malley had interrupted Claude only once when he seemed to change a timeline in the notes he had taken. The clarification offered by Claude made sense. In about an hour Mrs. Glavin had read the account she had written down in her steno pad. Except for two minor changes of words, Claude had agreed to the statement.

O'Malley had stayed in the interview room with Claude while Mrs. Glavin went to type up the report. The Inspector had offered Claude a few words of advice, "Claude, I sense that you are basically an honest person. However, you've allowed yourself to fall into a trap where one error of judgment leads to another until a whole other life begins to build around you. It has also become destructive. However, it was not what the investigators and news reporters had suspected in the hanging scenario that you had originally described. Claude, you lost the security of your job as Mr. Weigand's chauffeur, Mortimer was led to go into hiding leaving the confidence of his mentor and friend, Mr. Willard, President of the Whaling City National Bank, and the clandestine operation led by the FBI was put into jeopardy. Your dear friend and co-worker, Mrs. Moriarity, who had helped raise Mortimer Weigand and kept his household, has left the area and travelled to Maryland to join her daughter Maureen and young grandson, Patrick. This change in Mrs. Moriarity's life held some consoling and positive elements. However, they were not chosen but imposed on her by your actions."

Into the Dark

Chapter Twelve

Claude recalled leaving the downtown police station quite shaken but resolved that he would bring this **dark** chapter of his life to an end. As he walked down the front stairs of the station, he had automatically reached into his pocket to take out his package of Lucky Strikes. He stopped and looked at the red circle on the pack. Viewing a trash container adjacent to the stairs, he dropped the unfinished pack into the bin. He was determined to turn a new leaf.

For months now he had made multiple resolutions in his mind, only to see them dissolve in the moment of trial. He needed to reveal this entire episode to Anne. He was convinced of their love for each other. But would she be able to completely trust him again? On his bus ride back to the North End of the city he had begun to put his thoughts together. There was a part of him that wanted to soften the blow for Anne and also a part that wanted to provide an asylum for his ego.

He continued to struggle with himself. He had become quite proficient in covering his tracks. He had felt a strong temptation to continue along this streak of deceptions. Slowly he had to admit to himself that he needed to share with Anne the blunt story of his gambling, the covering of his losses by digging into their reserved funds and his theft of cash from Mortimer. As a result, all these self-deceits had finally led to Mortimer's frenzied plan to disappear under the guise of a homicide or suicide, with Claude playing a central role in the cover-up.

It finally hit him that the best way to relate this shameful tale to Anne was to keep as close as possible to the statement that had just been recorded at the police station. Detective Barrett had worked hard to get him to reveal the facts and not a story. Now he needed an opportunity to share this with Anne. Since they lived with Anne's parents, the prospect of doing this privately at home was slight. He was also now convinced that he couldn't afford himself the luxury of postponing the moment of disclosure with Anne. It had to happen that night.

The thought finally struck him that he would meet Anne as she exited the bus on the Avenue. He would invite her to go to sit on the benches in Brooklawn Park across from St. Joseph's Church. This was a special place between them. It was there that he had informed Anne of his enlisting in the Navy. Anne had been such a good sport. That day they had entered the Church and found comfort, and committed themselves to each other. Claude had to acknowledge to himself that he wasn't assured of a similar outcome.

Prior to meeting Anne at the bus stop near Labonte's Pharmacy, Claude went home to the apartment that he and Anne shared with his in-laws. Mrs. Saulnier was home. Claude informed her, "I'm planning to meet Anne at the bus stop and we'll probably go for a walk to the park. We might be a little late for supper."

Claude could almost sense the thoughts going through Mrs. Saulnier's head, "He's such a good boy. My lovely Anne couldn't have found a better one." The feeling of guilt just mushroomed inside him. As fearful as he was in facing his real self, he sensed in his inner soul that this was the moment of no return.

Claude wanted to pray but he found that even God couldn't be the one to take charge of his life. This was his own moment.

Claude recalled changing into a clean shirt that Anne had ironed for him. Dark stains of perspiration under his armpits had covered his old shirt. He felt rather poignantly the shame of his condition and maybe even disorder. Finally, he had succumbed to a basic prayer, "Jesus, help me."

Anne's eyes opened widely as she stepped off the bus and found Claude standing on the sidewalk. Claude had started by saying, "Do you mind walking over to the park? There's something I need to say." Claude quickly detected concern and anxiety creeping in on Anne.

Anne agreed, and held on to Claude's arm with all the strength she had. The perplexed and disparate feelings that both had experienced for quite a while now were making themselves known.

Claude found a park bench near the duck pond.

Claude wrapped his arms around Anne. He looked into her eyes and began his tale of deceit. Anne listened quietly as Claude told of his gambling at the croquet club, including that this was the reason he was home late for dinner on occasion. When Claude told her that he had taken from their savings to cover his losses, tears streamed down Anne's face. She asked him, "Why didn't you tell me?"

Claude answered truthfully, "I thought I could put the funds back before we needed them. That seemed to work for a while."

Anne in deep anguish had added, "This was all going on when I became pregnant and had my miscarriage. Oh, Claude. How could you?"

Claude suddenly became aware that his deceit had not only affected himself but the person he most loved in the whole world. "I'm so sorry," was all he could say.

The remainder of Claude's tale about his theft from Mr. Weigand and ensuing other divergent results in their lives didn't seem to affect Anne.

Anne had previously professed that she would be and was with him even when he lost his employment. She worked with him side by side. Together they could and would overcome every obstacle. Anne had cried out, "Oh, Claude! Why did you do this to me?"

After a long pause sitting on the park bench, Anne had finally said, "Let's go to the Church."

Together they had walked across the Avenue and up the stairs of the Church. Claude recalled the faint smell of incense and smoldering candles that filled the air. Anne led them to the small front altar of the Virgin. They knelt together before the statue. Eventually Anne looked up to Claude and had said, "Let's go home to supper. We'll work it out."

Into the Dark

Chapter Thirteen

Clara was the youngest of the Lepage girls and had graduated from St. Anthony's High School. She was now attending Kinyon-Campbell business school in the evenings and worked as a receptionist in a small family law office. She was hoping to one day become a para-professional. On Friday and Saturday nights she helped her brother at the fish and chip store. As with all the Lepages, she had lots of energy.

She looked to Anne who sat across the aisle in the bus and said, "I can't imagine what may have happened to little Andrew."

Anne aware that Claude was deep in thought glanced reassuringly at Clara saying, "Maybe he's been found by now. We'll soon know more when we get home."

"I hope so," answered Clara. "I would think they would have called us if things had changed."

When the threesome alighted from the bus, Clara quickly stepped ahead of Claude and Anne and hurried to the Lepage home down the street. The time was approaching 10 o'clock. She could see in her mind little Andrew pulling his red wagon up and down the street collecting the newspapers used at the restaurant.

Claude and Anne walked more slowly behind her. They were holding hands when Claude said, "I can't get away from the feeling that my past behavior has brought this possible calamity on the family."

Anne answered, "Oh, Claude. That's not healthy talk. You can't think that way. You made a mistake and it hurt me, but let's not let it consume you into a whirlpool of doubt and guilt. And don't put it on God. That's not His way."

When Claude and Anne entered the Lepage tenement, it was evident on Clara's face, who was being brought up to date on the situation, that matters had not improved. Clara was holding a hand to her mouth saying, "Oh, no. It's **dark** and cold out."

After a while Anne excused herself and announced that she was going to their apartment across the street, "I'm sure my mother and father must be worried." She also carried the receipts in her large hand bag and wanted to secure them in the locked box that had been nailed to the floor of their closet.

A few minutes later Al Lepage came into his parent's apartment. Prior to taking his Saturday evening bath and retiring for the night, he told Janet, "I'm going to make a quick visit downstairs and see if there are any new developments. I hope my brothers and I can come up with a plan."

After a few exchanges, Al asked his brother Claude and Joseph to join him in the front parlor. "This is ridiculous. We need to do something." Joseph almost yelled, "Please, what can we do to help?"

Al proposed the following, "I thought that we could go house to house and see what we can find. It's too late now. We would only alarm the neighbors. However, we can make some phone calls. Joseph most of your young friends are most likely still up this hour of the night. Try to reach them at home or places you know they hang out on a Saturday night. Let them know your nephew is missing and give them a description that Louise gave us of the man. With Martha's help Janet is trying to come up with a sketch of the man. As you know Janet is very artistic."

Claude volunteered, "I can call the croquet club and ask that they pass the word to the members. They stay open past eleven on Saturday."

"Then let's try to get some sleep and be ready to go to the 6 o'clock Mass," advised Al. "We'll ask the priest to announce at all the Masses about Andrew's disappearance and ask for assistance and prayers."

Joseph nodded but seemed disappointed in the plan. His pent up anxiety required more activity and said, "After Mass what about the three of us each take a street and do as you first suggested and go knocking on doors? It will be day light by then."

"That's what I was thinking too," agreed Al. "Joseph you can take the street to the north. It wasn't that long ago that you played in the school yard nearby. Claude you can take this street and I'll go one block south. I have a few bread customers and travel up and down that street often enough to recognize anything out of the ordinary. I hope Janet will be able to make some flyers with the sketch of the man that we can bring along with us. Someone may recognize him."

It wasn't much but rather than just waiting for something to happen, the plan of contacting people in the area might produce some results.

When Al returned to his apartment, Janet showed him the sketch that Martha claimed to capture Louise's description of the man. He knew that Janet could do it. "That's great, Janet," said an admiring Al. "Do you think you can make some flyers, maybe a dozen or so? Claude, Joseph and I have agreed to go to the six o'clock Mass tomorrow morning and then canvas the neighborhood. The sketch of the man and some brief details could be helpful in triggering someone's memory. We can leave one on the door of the church, at the drug store…"

54

Janet agreed that she could reproduce more of the sketches. "I have a whole pad of artist paper," she said as she flipped through the still blank pages."

Martha volunteered, "I can write up some of the details that happened today and write it below the sketch. My script isn't as good as Janet's but should do."

Janet responded, "I have a bold pen in that holder that will make it easier for people to see and read."

Into the Dark

Book Four

Into the Dark

Book Four

Chapter Fourteen

The search goes on...

On his way back to his office at the central precinct, Chief Inspector Daniel O'Malley made a quick stop at his home. He had already missed the family evening meal but wanted to reassure himself that his two girls, Margaret and Julia, were home safely with their mother.

His wife Maria greeted him with her welcoming kiss as he walked into the front room. Daniel inquired, "Are the girls at home?"

Maria answered, "Margaret is in her room studying diligently as usual. She has a trigonometry exam on Monday. Maybe you can help her once you've eaten and settled in."

Daniel informed Maria, "I won't be staying. I was just checking in. What about Julia?"

"Oh," answered Maria, "she should be home shortly. The ballet group that she recently joined had an extra rehearsal this evening. They will be performing "Peter Pan" soon after Easter. She's one of the dancers in three background scenes. I watched her practice earlier this afternoon. She's taken to this new stage performance with great energy and seriousness. You should see her concentration as they practice their steps and moves. She told us at supper that she would love to play the role of Tinker Bell someday. She especially likes the attitude that her friend Madison brings to the role in this production. She feels that she could even bring more striking innovations to the role. She's quite the girl."

Again Daniel inquired, "How is she getting home?"

Maria informed Daniel, "Bev Medeiros picked her up after supper and brought Julia and her daughter Melissa to the rehearsal. They should be back shortly."

Maria sensed Daniel's concern and asked, "Are you alright? You seem anxious."

Daniel tried to reassure her. He wasn't ready to share the case of the missing boy with her.

"Do you have time to have something to eat?" Maria asked.

"No," answered Daniel. "I just wanted to check in. It could be a long evening at the precinct."

Maria insisted, "Let me put some of our evening meal together for you. You can nibble on it when time permits."

As Maria turned to go to the kitchen to fetch Daniel's food, both heard the familiar bouncing steps of Julia in the front hall.

Julia ran up to her father and just hugged and gave him a long kiss on the lips. "Oh, Daddy you're home. I was so excited to see your car in front of the house."

She looked at him and wondered aloud, "You have your coat on. Are you going off?"

Daniel sadly answered, "We're working on an important case. I just came by to make sure you were fine. Your mother just told me of this extra ballet rehearsal you had tonight. You'll have to tell me all about it tomorrow."

Hearing the commotion downstairs, Margaret broke away from her studies and joined them in the front room. She greeted her father with a warm, quick kiss on the cheek. Maria came in with a package and said, "It won't be as tasty cold but it will sustain your strength." Looking keenly at Daniel, she asked, "You haven't eaten all day, have you?"

Daniel shrugged. "I must get going." They all hugged together.

Into the Dark

Chapter Fifteen

Before leaving the scene of the missing Lepage boy, Inspector O'Malley called and spoken with the Police Chief Luke Guerney. He briefed him on the unsuccessful search of the neighborhood and that the evidence collected so far probably pointed to an abduction.

O'Malley informed the chief, "We have a good description of a person of interest. I want to review files and put together a composite that we can give to our patrol officers as soon as possible. Can you assign Detective Paul Griffin to the case?Have him join me at the station. I should be there shortly. Tell him it could be a long night."

Detective Paul Griffin was an unmarried young man in his early thirties. He had quickly come up the ranks and had become a detective in the New Bedford Police Department about a year before Detective Joseph Barrett's retirement from the force.

Inspector O'Malley was still becoming accustomed to Detective Griffin's work habits and personality. The retired Joseph Barrett had become as familiar to O'Malley as an old shoe.

It was a little after 9 pm that O'Malley finally settled into his office. The station was its usual quiet early on a Saturday night. The front desk officer had greeted O'Malley, "I hear you're putting in an all-nighter." The evening shift patrolmen had already been briefed and had gone on their assignments. Except for two booking officers, who normally got quite busy on a typical Saturday night, the building was quiet.

O'Malley closed the window of his office. When he had left earlier in the day the heat of the sun entering the room had made it rather stifling. But now a cold, damp breeze was hitting his back. O'Malley started to complete his report, especially trying to faithfully capture the description of the would be perpetrator.

As he was putting the finishing touches to his notes, the sound of singing and humming could be heard approaching down the hall to his office. Before long, the short, physically fit Detective Paul Griffin was at Inspector O'Malley's door. With a big smile, he announced, "Reporting for duty, sir. I'm at your service."

"Come in," invited O'Malley. "We'll start working in here."

Paul Griffin put a paper bag on the side table and informed O'Malley, "I brought a couple of sandwiches. I haven't eaten since lunch time. My mother reached me at the bowling alley telling me that the Chief had called me at home assigning me to your case and to report ASAP."

"Oh," continued Paul, "I hope you don't mind. I brought my portable radio. The Celtics are on tonight. They're playing the Lakers in Minneapolis."

O'Malley reflected on the very different atmosphere that surrounded working with this young man. He responded, "No problem. Just keep the volume down."

Paul picked up the radio and plugged it into the wall socket, saying, "This will save the batteries and usually it gives a clearer sound." After some squawking noises as Paul searched for the Boston station, the strong sound of the announcer filled the room. Paul lowered the volume and asked, "Is this OK?'

Inspector O'Malley nodded. He then briefed Paul about the case of the young boy who had gone missing and feared abducted in one of the French Canadian neighborhoods in the north end of the city. He instructed the detective, "Go to the files and bring back here any case files that relate to missing children, kidnappings even rape and the discovery of bodies of young children. Go back six months. No let's make that a year. Sometime these cases are repeated at a particular time of year or some other regular pattern. In the meantime, I'm going to follow up with the neighboring police departments and see if they've uncovered anything helpful to share with us. Earlier the Chief had alerted them of our situation and that we would be seeking their assistance."

As Paul Griffin exited the office, he stopped briefly to listen to the voice of Red Auerbach being interviewed at half time. "I'll be right back with the files." He didn't know the score but he was eager to return to the office and pick up some of the highlights of the second half. Tommy Heinsohn, who had joined the Celtics this year, came from Paul Griffin's Alma Mata, Holy Cross College. As a new forward he joined another already famous alumnus, Bob Cousy.

Paul Griffin made three trips with his arms filled with files that related to young children. He placed them on the long work table and somewhat reluctantly decided to clear the table by putting the radio on the floor. He was beginning to sense the importance of the case.

The Inspector instructed, "These are some of the items of interest that we are looking for in the files – a white male, anywhere between 30 and 50 years of age, maybe even older, a round face and bald with dark hair on the sides, who wears glasses. He was described by the boy's sister as wearing a plaid winter jacket with "Sunday" pants not work pants, this is Saturday. So he is probably someone who works in some type of a professional position."

Paul Griffin questioned, "In your earlier briefing you mentioned that this man had invited both the young girl and boy to follow him. So we are not just looking for the abduction of young male. Am I correct?"

O'Malley agreed, "That's a good observation, Paul." Sitting down to one side of the work table, he added, "If we find anything in these files that has any resemblance to these points of interest, let's put them aside for now. We'll study them together later."

Both men worked quietly. O'Malley was impressed by the young detective's concentration. He didn't seem to be distracted by the basketball game in the background. Even when the announcer's voice celebrated the flashy moves of Bob Cousy, Paul continued with his task.

Together they had set aside over a dozen files. O'Malley suggested, "Let's take some time to eat before we continue. My wife packed me some leftovers from the family supper."

Paul readily agreed, "I'm going to get a coke from the cooler in the hall. Do you want anything, a cup of coffee?"

"No," answered O'Malley. "My stomach doesn't agree with coffee this late in the day. I'll make myself a cup of tea."

Into the Dark

Chapter Sixteen

While eating the two men listened attentively to the game. Bill Russell at 6'9", who was in his first year with the Celtics, was proving to be a dominant defender at his post under the basket. It was becoming almost routine for him to block a shot and, with a quick flick pass to the speedy Bob Cousy, it would result in an easy layup.

The game seemed to be well in the hands of the Celtics. The Lakers were only a shell of their former selves. A couple of years earlier George Mikan who dominated the boards had empowered the team to consistently win the Western Division of the NBA. After beating the New York Knicks twice in a row to win the Finals, the tag of Dynasty was added to their label. However, a few years earlier due to bad knees, George Mikan had been forced to retire.

O'Malley suggested, "You look over the files I set aside and I'll review those you selected. Then we'll share our findings."

O'Malley was itching to find a lead in the case but didn't want to waste precious time and effort following a wrong lead.

Detective Paul Griffin set one file aside. He looked up to see the Inspector coming to the last of his files. "I think I found something," stated an excited young man.

O'Malley questioned, "Can you give me your findings?"

Paul Griffin took a breath. "This file contains a case that occurred about a year ago," he started.

O'Malley quickly took out his note pad and started to make entries of the details of Paul's discoveries.

"This man was reported of suspicious behavior on different occasions by mothers who either waited for their children outside of their elementary schools or watched over their children at a local park," started Paul. "He was brought in for questioning at the south end precinct. We don't have a photo but his description has enough similarities to make him a suspect."

O'Malley asked, "Can you relate what the file contains about this man's description? I'll write them down."

Paul related, "He is described as middle age, balding and somewhat heavy. The word fat is not used."

O'Malley further inquired, "Are there any references to him wearing eye glasses?"

Paul fingered through the file and eventually stated, "No. The statement of the women who reported his lurking manners around their children didn't make any reference to him wearing glasses. Our men who interviewed him don't make any such reference either. Barry Lynch was one of our guys. We were in the same class at the Academy. We bump into each other at the bowling alley. He's a member of the police union league. He may remember the case, but it's over a year ago."

O'Malley finally asked, "Was there anything in particular that made you focus on this file? You seemed excited."

"Yes," answered Paul. "I've been waiting to share it with you. The man owns a grey van. The guy gave his name as Charles Piedmont. He was released after questioning. They had no evidence to hold him. The officers advised him to stay away from places where children gather and that he was on their watch list. However, before they closed the file, the officers searched the Registry of Motor Vehicles' files and added that he owned a **dark green** van. It's the last entry."

O'Malley asked, "Do we have an address?"

"The Charles Piedmont vehicle was listed at 2043 State Street just above Giammalvo's Market on Purchase Street. It's part of the Acushnet Heights section of the city. I used to patrol that area when I was a foot soldier," added Paul.

Inspector O'Malley deliberated briefly and came up with a strategy, saying to his detective, "Every moment in a child abduction case is extremely critical if we hope to find the victim alive and unharmed. I'm going to call the night captain at your former precinct and ask him to send two patrol cars there and to wait for you to arrive on the scene."

Paul jumped up immediately and put on his coat. As he wrapped a long scarf around his neck, O'Malley continued, "It's approaching midnight but we can't wait to pursue this lead until tomorrow morning. Be courteous but persistent. If Charles Piedmont lives there now or even lived there in the past, try your utmost to be allowed to search the property. We don't have a search warrant but I'll contact the Chief and a local magistrate. We have good cause to search the property. This type of perpetrator often hides their victims for a while prior to disposing of them."

O'Malley was being starkly honest with his new detective but shivered inside as he forced himself to face the terrible possibilities of the case.

Into the Dark

Chapter Seventeen

A groggy police chief answered the telephone on the lampstand near his bed, "Luke Guerney here."

When the chief heard Inspector O'Malley's distraught request, he immediately swung out of bed and told O'Malley, "I'll contact Judge Green. I know he's in town this weekend. We had dinner together Friday evening. I have his home phone number. If he needs any particulars for the warrant, I'll have him contact you at the precinct. Stay close to the phone for the next half hour."

Christine Guerney had awakened and looked inquisitively at her husband, "What's wrong? Do you have to go to the police station?"

"No," answered Luke. "I have to make a call. I'll go make it on the kitchen phone." As much as Luke wanted to share some of the incidents of his work, both he and his wife had agreed that he would keep such information to himself until he made them public at a news conference."

While waiting for the call, O'Malley scrutinized the file one more time. He found a piece of information that added confusion to the case. The man who had identified himself as Charles Piedmont had given an address on Walnut Street in the center of the city. This conflicted with the address where the vehicle in question was registered.

When Judge Arthur Green called looking for specifics to justify the issue of a search warrant, the Inspector provided such information about the residence on State Street. He then added the finding of an additional address on Walnut Street, and requested that the search warrant include this location as well.

Judge Green considered briefly and said, "I can't justify such an open ended search. You have given me sufficient evidence in reference to the State Street address. A vehicle has been part of your investigation. The police files substantiate the existence of a similar vehicle registered to a person under some suspicion of similar heinous activities. Time is of the essence. Remember, Inspector, this is a warrant to search, not to accuse the person in question."

O'Malley thanked the Judge and immediately called Detective Paul Griffin, saying, "We have a warrant to search the State Street address. You can so inform the owner and begin a search. If they insist on seeing the warrant, you'll have to wait. I'll get it to you as soon as I can."

In the meantime, O'Malley and one of the booking officers went to the Walnut Street address not far from the central police station. A quick view of the building gave evidence that it was a rooming house. There was a small sign on the exterior.

"This presents a problem," stated the Inspector. "I wonder if the landlord resides on the property?"

Officer Bob Ferreira commented, "I know this place. On my day shifts I've gotten to know the woman who manages the rooming house. Mrs. Laura Nunes runs a clean, no nonsense establishment. She lives in the rear first floor apartment."

As they approached the rear entrance, Bob Ferreira pointed to a shadow on the far end of the stoop that extended the whole width of the building. "That's one of Laura's tenants sleeping it off. They know better than to enter the house when they are drunk."

After a few knocks on the rear doorway, a light went on in a room facing them. Then in a few minutes the light on the porch went on. O'Malley saw a middle aged woman putting on her housecoat and approaching the door. There was no smile on her face even when she saw the police uniform on Bob Ferreira.

"How may I help you?" she asked quite disturbed.

Bob introduced himself and then, "This is Inspector O'Malley. We are under time constraints in the investigation of a case. It's important."

Inspector O'Malley interjected, "Mrs. Nunes, we are looking for a man who gave us this as his address about a year ago. He gave us his name as Charles Piedmont."

Laura Nunes answered quickly, "I've never had a tenant by that name. Never! I know my people."

O'Malley feared that would be the case. "Could we bother you for a few more minutes?" asked O'Malley. "We would like to go over a description of the man in question and see if you recall such a person."

"OK, come in," answered Mrs. Nunes. In the hallway to her apartment, they passed a stairway closest to the exterior door going to the second floor and a closed door just beyond on the same left side of the hallway.

O'Malley questioned, "Is that a closet?"

Laura Nunes turned back and said, "No. It's a stairway to the cellar." She gave every air of being totally disgusted by these fumbling, intrusive visitors.

Inspector O'Malley had expected that answer. He had been in enough of these wooden structures of the city and was familiar with the design. He just needed some confirmation.

Laura Nunes invited the two men into her apartment. It was very neat but the furniture of the small living room was well worn.

Laura did not invite her visitors to sit. She quickly asked, "What does your man look like? Hurry now. I need my sleep. This is already Sunday morning and my house guests expect a good breakfast."

O'Malley gave Mrs. Nunes a description, realizing how generic it was to anyone hearing it. He emphasized, "He was described as being bald, with dark hair toward the back of his head. He had a round face and somewhere between 30 and 50 years of age. He wore glasses and wore suit pants not work pants."

Laura thought a while, "Boys, that describes a lot of people around this neighborhood. However, you said that this person gave you this address about a year ago. I never forget a face. It's important in my business."

Laura continued, "A man fitting your description has roomed here over the last few years. Usually, only a month or two at a time. He keeps to himself. He pays on time and I welcome him back if I have a room available. He doesn't wear the work pants that the majority of my tenants' wear. I don't know the nature of his work. He doesn't seem to follow any regular work hours. He registers as Charles Peruzzi. Is he in any trouble?'

O'Malley responded, "All I can say is that he is a person of interest in one of our current cases. Is he living here now?"

Laura's natural curiosity was awakened and answered, "No. He moved out at the end of the month."

"Any idea where he may have gone?" asked O'Malley.

"No," answered Laura. "He appears on the scene, as I said, quite unexpectedly and leaves once the terms of his rent is over.

There is no explanation ever given to me of where he may go. He never receives any mail here so there is no reason to have it forwarded to him."

O'Malley suddenly remembered that Louise had stated something about the look of anger of the man's face. He ventured another question, "Did he ever express anger with you or the other boarders?"

Mrs. Nunes answered, "He was always very courteous with me. Of course, if he followed the house rules, which he did, I never had reason to get on him. However, he could be quite disagreeable to some of the tenants. As I said, he keeps to himself. If a boarder was too inquisitive or asked to enter his room, he flatly turned them away. A new boarder would only try that once. The look on Charles' face will do that to you."

O'Malley continued, "Is there anything else that you can think of that may help us locate this man?"

"Yes," answered Mrs. Nunes. "I've been wanting to mention that I never saw Charles wear any type of eyeglasses."

O'Malley pondered on that comment and then added, "Do any of your tenants have access to the cellar?"

"Only when they store something down there," answered Mrs. Nunes. "Of course I always accompany them to a dry spot in the rear of the cellar. The door of the basement is always kept locked and I have the only key." Laura pointed to a set of keys hanging near the frame of the door.

Into the Dark

Chapter Eighteen

Detective Paul Griffin met the police officers in front of a darkened large single family home. In its day it would have been quite impressive. It contrasted with the multi-family residences to the north heading toward Weld Street.

Paul recognized one of the officers, Gus Silvia. Gus introduced his partner, Bill Belliveau. Briefly Paul related the reason for their presence at this hour of the night. He asked, "Are either of you familiar with the residents in this house?"

Gus said, "I've been working this precinct for over twenty years and we've never been called out here for any disturbance. It may look empty and deserted but we've seen people coming in and out on occasion." Gus' partner agreed.

Paul informed these men, "I've just got word on my way here that a judge has issued a warrant to search the premises. Let's get started."

Detective Paul Griffin instructed Gus, "Go around to the back of the house and cover the rear entrance for now. Bill and I will try to awaken the occupants."

Gus observed as he went down a driveway using his flashlight that it was made of cement that was broken and cracked. He had to be careful not to stumble. It led to an unattached one car garage. There was a well-worn path that led from the back entrance of the house to a side door in the garage. He took up his post observing both entries and shut off his flashlight.

Meanwhile, Detective Griffin sent Officer Belliveau to the right side of the house and said, "Keep an eye on that side."

Paul climbed up the five rickety stairs to the large front porch. The street lights provided enough illumination so that he could avoid a broken board that led to the front door. An antique fixture was centered right into the middle just beneath what used to be a fancy leaded decorated window. Most of the glass was broken and covered with a board. Something that resembled a dirty towel covered the interior of the window. Paul twisted the mechanism and he could hear the strong sound of the bell ringing in the door. He waited a few minutes and whispering to Officer Belliveau standing at the front edge of the building, "Any lights coming on?" "No," came the reply.

Paul turned the bell with more determination. He thought, "Someone has to be a very heavy sleeper not to hear this entrance bell. Or maybe no one is at home."

Having received no response, Detective Griffin instructed Bill Belliveau, "Keep an eye on the front of the house while I go back to see if Gus has observed anything."

Detective Paul Griffin carefully made his way to the rear of the building. Officer Gus Silveira observed the light coming down the driveway. As he came out of the shadows, Paul's flashlight picked up the outline of the officer.

The detective asked, "Did any lights come on when I was ringing the bell at the front door?"

"No," answered Gus. "No lights, no activity, no noise."

Gus pointed, "I found this well-worn path between the house and the garage. Someone has been around here. Maybe they live in the rear of the house and didn't hear the bell. I didn't hear it from my position."

Detective Griffin suggested, "Before I announce myself at the rear door, let's take a peek into the garage."

Gus pointed his flashlight into the garage using the small dirty window in the side door and said, "I really can't see anything. There's some kind of a covering on the inside of the window. Shall I try the door?"

Griffin reviewed quickly in his mind the rules and limitations that applied to a search warrant. He was anxious to discover whether the **dark green** van in the case was in the garage. He told Gus, "OK."

Gus turned the rusty door knob and found it unlocked. He was able to push it open.

Griffin cautioned Gus, "Don't enter the building. Just shine your light into it and see if there is a vehicle parked inside."

Gus replied, "There's no car in the garage." Streaming his light deeper into its recesses said, "There's a lot of stuff in the rear of the garage. But there's enough empty space in the front to make room for a vehicle."

"That's enough for now," said Griffin. "Close the door and let us try the rear entrance to the house. We may be able to awaken someone. If there is anyone at home."

Repeated knocks on the rear door didn't bring anyone to the door. Griffin gingerly tried the door handle but it was securely locked.

Griffin said, "Let's go back to the front and consider our options with Bill. We don't want to overstep our bounds. I may want to call Inspector O'Malley and confer with him before we proceed any further."

Into the Dark

Chapter Nineteen

After their visit to Mrs. Nunes' rooming house, Inspector O'Malley and Officer Bob Ferreira returned to the downtown police station. The place was a beehive of activity. It was a typical Saturday night. The benches in the hallway were filled mostly with men who had partied to excess at the local bars. There were two women sitting further down the corridor. One was dressed in clothes that would distinguish her as she wandered the area of the waterfront. The other was a gray haired woman whose long night gown could be seen under a threadbare brown coat.

Gus asked, "If it's alright with you. I better get back to my duties. There's a lot of processing work to do."

O'Malley gave him the OK. As he passed the front desk on his way to his office, the officer held out an envelope and said, "Someone just dropped this off for you. They said it was important."

The Inspector glanced at the contents of the envelope. It contained a carefully typed copy of a search warrant for the residence on State Street signed by Judge Robert Green.

Instead of returning to his office, he exited the police station and drove himself to State Street with the search warrant. He found Detective Griffin conferring with his police officers.

O'Malley held out the envelope and announced, "I have the search warrant. How are things going on here?"

Detective Paul Griffin brought him up to date, "There doesn't seem to be anyone at home. There's a garage at the back of the house. Its side door wasn't locked and we looked into it but didn't enter the building."

O'Malley quickly asked, "Was there a vehicle parked in the garage?"

"No," answered Griffin. Officer Gus Silveira added, "But there is enough empty space to park a vehicle."

Young detective Griffin said, "I was getting ready to call you and seek your advice as to how to proceed from here. I don't want to compromise a probable case by doing something that would not be admissible in court."

Inspector O'Malley instructed the men before him, "This warrant authorizes us to conduct a search of a person, location or vehicle for evidence of a crime and to confiscate any evidence we find. Normally, we wouldn't intrude onto someone's personal property without their knowledge. But since no one has responded to your preliminary inquiries, and we have sufficient evidence that a crime of abduction has been committed on a young and innocent child, this warrant allows us to search the premises."

The group strategized for a while and agreed that Officer Bill Belliveau would keep his post at the front of the structure and Officer Gus Silveira would cover the back. Inspector O'Malley and Detective Griffin would first investigate the garage.

O'Malley went to his vehicle and produced two pairs of rubber type gloves. He offered one to the detective saying, "As you know we have to be careful not to compromise the scene."

Inspector O'Malley equipped with Officer Belliveau's flashlight opened the side door of the garage. He and Detective Griffin entered the dark building. Detective Griffin first pointed out, "There's a fresh oil spot in the parking space. A vehicle was here not that long ago."

As they went deeper into the interior of the garage, they found all kinds of debris and boxes. A few tools were on a small bench. Behind some stacked boxes O'Malley's flashlight lighted on a mattress in the corner. He pointed it out to the Detective and said, "I think we have found where someone sleeps. Look, there is evidence that that person eats and drinks here as well."

Detective Griffin informed O'Malley, "Gus Silveira observed a frequently used path between the garage and the rear door of the house. Whoever uses this place also accesses the house."

O'Malley stated, "You mentioned that the rear door is locked."

"That's right," answered Griffin.

"Did you try any of the windows," asked O'Malley.

"No," answered Griffin. "I wasn't sure how far to proceed in the search."

"Let's see if we can find a window that opens," stated O'Malley. "I would rather not break down the door. But time is of the essence. So we'll see."

The second window on the rear porch that Paul Griffin tried was unlocked and moved slightly upward but became stuck. Paul turned to O'Malley, "Should I put some muscle into it?"

O'Malley gave his assent.

The young detective was short but evidently worked out regularly. Standing near the building with his legs slightly bent at the knees, he put his two hands within the space and pushed upward. At first the window resisted. Griffin jiggled the window a bit and again tried to lift it. It resisted but eventually became free from some obstruction and opened to its full height.

"Should I enter?" asked Paul.

Yes," answered O'Malley.

With the use of his flashlight Paul looked into the room and said, "It's a small kitchen. There's a sink just inside the window with some dirty pots and dishes."

O'Malley cautioned Griffin to be careful. "Once you are in the house, see if you can unlock the rear door."

Griffin made some noise as he climbed through the window, over the sink and finally to the floor. However, nothing fell to the floor to announce his entry. He found his way to the rear entry and unlocked the door.

Griffin pointed out to O'Malley, "This door was locked from the inside and not by a key. I had to slide this bolt in order to open the door. Someone could be in the house."

Into the Dark

Chapter Twenty

Inspector O'Malley stated, "Let's announce our presence and see if anyone responds."

In his loud deep voice Detective Paul Griffin shouted out, "This is the police department. We are seeking to speak with the occupants."

No one answered or came forward. O'Malley instructed Griffin, "Take out your firearm and we'll start a search of the house."

O'Malley's flashlight focused upward at a heavy string hanging from the ceiling of the kitchen. "Let's see if there is any electricity in the house."

Nothing happened. With the aid of their flashlights the two men entered the adjoining room. It looked like it used to be a formal dining room. A large table with tons of stuff on it centered the room. There was only one dining room chair with a broken leg leaning against the right wall. A built in wall cabinet contained a few odd pieces of china – mostly broken. Wallpaper hung down in strips between two exterior windows.

Further into the front of the house, they discovered two large rooms adjacent to each other with the front entry door at the center. Paul Griffin shined his light on the bolt that helped secure the door from the inside and said, "There's the front doorbell that we could clearly hear from the outside."

Except for some debris, both rooms did not contain any furniture.

A stairway to the second floor was opposite the front door. Paul looked at O'Malley, "Shall we?" When O'Malley nodded in the affirmative, Paul proceeded up the stairs with his gun pointing forward in his right hand and the flashlight in his left hand joining together. He took a deep breath as he went up the stairs with O'Malley behind him. Daniel O'Malley as Chief Homicide Inspector never carried a firearm on his person when in the field. He always qualified with high marks at the firing range. He relied on trained police officers to accompany him during such an investigation. However, this was not the customary experience for the Inspector. Normally, he would appear on a crime scene after it had been secured. The expediency required in this case didn't allow for that luxury.

They discovered four doorways, all closed. One room contained a broken bed frame, just with a flat spring still attached to the frame. The door to the closet was open and except for some stuff packed into one corner it was empty. The other room contained an old sewing machine. It was foot powered. A door, presumably to a closet, was shut tight. Paul Griffin trained his firearm on the opening as O'Malley quickly turned the handle and opened the door. Again it was empty except for some clutter.

The larger room to the left of the stairway contained some pieces of furniture. A classic settee covered with some deep colored material was positioned so as to look outside in the front of the building. There were no doors in this room.

As the men were approaching the last room at the top of the stairs, they could hear a steady noise inside. Both looked at each other. This door opened inward. Paul stood at attention and O'Malley tried the door handle, it turned. Whispering O'Malley said, "On the count of two, I'll throw open the door."

They discovered a rather large bathroom. The noise they had heard was that of water dripping from a faucet of the large claw style bathtub. A heavy rusty stain shone in their light. This water had been dripping for a long time.

O'Malley and Griffin returned to the kitchen area where they had started their search. It was becoming evident that the building was empty and abandoned. A door at one end of the kitchen hadn't been explored. It looked like it could be a pantry.

Just as Paul went to open the door, O'Malley cautioned, "Let's not get careless."

They returned to the protocol of O'Malley opening the door with Paul Griffin training his gun on the entryway.

What they discovered surprised both of them. What might have been a large pantry had been turned into a bedroom. It had no windows. A bed with mattress and linens was to one side. There was a small dresser and on the wall hung neat dress suits and a few ties. The dresser contained clean underwear and socks, plus ironed shirts. A ribbon on the shirts indicated that a local laundry had pressed and packaged the shirts.

Detective Griffin pointing to the shirts said, "This should help identify the occupant."

O'Malley took a clear bag from the pocket of his trench coat and said, "Carefully remove the band from the package and place it in the evidence bag. We'll contact the laundry for information about the person who brought in the shirts."

As they were leaving the room, Paul Griffin noticed that a door had been hidden from their view by the door that opened into the room. A definite unease came over him. The search that had become rather routine was again filled with apprehension given the discoveries made in this room.

Behind the door they discovered a stairway that led downward beneath the structure. Prior to descending Paul used his flash light to examine the stairs carefully. They had come this far without incident. This wasn't the time to become reckless and injure himself.

O'Malley flashed his light around the entrance and pointed out, "Paul, there's a light on the wall. Pull the string. This light may work."

Again a couple of repeated pulls on the string didn't produce any light. Paul reached up to the bulb and discovered it was loose. A few twist and suddenly Paul was blinded by its light.

Cautiously Paul proceeded down the stairway. The light above cast shadows below, so he trained his flash light downward and to the opening on the left. The right side of the stairway was up against the foundation of the building. The air from below was cold and damp.

O'Malley stayed in the room and poked his head into the kitchen to assure himself that it was still empty and no one had crept up behind them. He thought to himself, "We don't want to find ourselves locked in the cellar."

Paul Griffin called back up the stairway, "No one's down here. It's a rather small room and pretty tidy too. There's a door leading out." With some excitement in his voice, Paul continued, "There's also a bolt on this door but it's open. I think we've found how our occupant entered and exited the building. I'll investigate further."

Paul opened the door and found a stairway that led upward. The cold fresh air of the early Sunday morning greeted him. It was still dark outdoors. The stairway led to a tall space beneath the back porch. Paul was greeted by Gus Silveira who had been standing watch at the rear of the old house. Gus announced, "As I waited, I had time to scrutinize the path between the garage and the house. It led to this far end of the porch and not to the stairs of the back porch."

O'Malley could hear the conversation between the two men outdoors. The acoustics provided a sort of a surround sound. The still open window in the kitchen carried the sound as well as a deep echo that came from up the cellar stairway. He joined the men in the back of the yard. He instructed, "Paul, secure the building. I'll have a team examine the property and house thoroughly once we have daybreak. Meet me in the front of the house. Gus, keep watch out back until the team arrives. I'm going out front to confer with Officer Belliveau."

Officer Bill Belliveau excitedly approached the Inspector. He started, "I have been waiting to tell you something. Someone drove up to the house less than a half hour ago. It looked like the vehicle was slowing down to enter the driveway. All of a sudden it straightened out and drove quickly down the street. He couldn't have seen me. I was in the shadows and the lights of the car didn't penetrate my position. However, when I turned back to the house I noticed lights moving in the rooms upstairs. The driver must have seen them."

O'Malley shrugged his shoulders. He asked, "Were you able to identify the vehicle?"

Officer Bill answered, "I couldn't make out the make and model. But the streetlight on the corner captured a dark colored van."

Inspector O'Malley was becoming ever more confident that they were on the right path.

Into the Dark

Book Five

Into the Dark

Book Five

Chapter Twenty-one

Going forward...

Inspector O'Malley instructed Detective Paul Griffin to stay at the site on State Street with the two police officers. "I'll send two additional men to assist you in searching and cataloguing your findings," informed O'Malley. "It may take some time to get them together on an early Sunday morning. You might start by doing a more thorough search of the garage. There are no windows on the garage doors facing the front so the light shouldn't be observed from the street. But instruct Bill Belliveau to be especially vigilant. Our suspect may return and we have no knowledge as to whether he is capable of violence."

O'Malley returned to the main headquarters of the New Bedford Police Department a little before 3 o'clock. A cold mist was blowing in from the waterfront. A dim wisp of a moon was setting in the west below the heavier clouds above. He thought to himself, "Once the fog burns off, we might have a nice day." His joints ached as he climbed the stairs of the police station. He hadn't pulled an all-nighter in quite a while.

With the assistance of the officer at the front desk, O'Malley identified two men from the roster who were on call. The activity in the station was quieting down. The hallway benches were empty. He was sure that the holding cells contained those sleeping it off for their own safety and others held in captivity in order to safeguard the public. A judge would dispose of these cases later in the day.

O'Malley awakened both men and instructed them to meet Detective Griffin at the State Street residence. He told them, "We have a warrant to search the premises. Paul Griffin will fill you in when you get there. Swiftness in processing the material is critical."

Daniel O'Malley needed some quiet time to process the findings of the evening. He would have liked to have the crafty old Joe Barrett around to bounce off the material. He hoped Joe was enjoying his retirement in upstate New York with his daughter and family.

The file that Paul Griffin had identified had produced some striking information. The suspect had given his name as Charles Piedmont but with his address at the rooming house on Walnut Street. There he had registered as Charles Perruzi. The vehicle in question, a dark van, was registered to a Charles Piedmont at the State Street address.

Young Andrew's sister, Louise, had recognized that the man wore "Sunday" trousers and not work pants. The secretive room that was discovered at the State Street residence contained only business type suits and clothing. Mrs. Laura Nunes had also indicated that her boarder wore suit type pants. O'Malley thought to himself, "There seems to be enough indication that Charles Piedmont and Charles Perruzi are one and the same person. But why would a Charles Piedmont, living alone in a large broken-down home on State Street, on occasion take up residence as a lodger at Mrs. Nunes' boarding house?"

Bending back in his desk chair and looking blankly at the ceiling, he conjectured, "There might be some connection between this strange activity and the suspicious behavior that originally brought the man to the authority's attention as described in the files and the present apparent abduction of Andrew."

First, he needed to follow up on some leads. Reviewing the file intently O'Malley affirmed his recollections, "The man had been interviewed at the south end precinct. The file mentions mothers reporting possible dubious behavior around elementary schools and at a local park." This behavior had been reported by mothers at more than one school location. Were they all in the south end of the city? The file did not explicitly state that as a fact. The Hazelwood Park in the south end of the city had been identified in the report.

Andrew and Louise lived in the north end of the city. Had anyone reported suspicious activity at one of the schools in that part of the city? Paul Griffin had mentioned that his classmate at the Police Academy, Barry Lynch had been listed as an arresting officer in the case. It was worth a call. Dawn still hadn't broken but police personnel were aware that they could be needed at any time of day or night.

"The Lynch's residence," answered a gruff male voice. "That's my son you're looking for. I'll get him for you. Hold on."

O'Malley identified himself and the reason for this inconvenient call. Barry answered, "Happy to be of service, sir. I remember the case but the details are rather foggy. I couldn't be specific about the schools in question. But Detective Tony Giberti did the interviewing. He might remember."

"Before I hang up," queried O'Malley. "You are listed in the report as the arresting officer. Do you remember where you made that arrest?"

"Yes, I do," answered Barry. "It was outside the Congdon School on Hemlock Street toward the south end of the city."

O'Malley found Tony Giberti's telephone number in the police department's Rolodex. He called the home number and was informed that Detective Giberti was on a case but probably at the south end station at this hour. O'Malley apologized for this early morning disruption.

Tony Giberti also remembered the case. He informed O'Malley, "Before Barry arrested Charles Piedmont we had quite a number of reports about a man of his description loitering around places where children naturally gather. As to the schools in question, reports were from all over the city."

O'Malley asked, "Did the reports include schools in the north end of the city?"

"Oh, yes," answered the detective. "I remember the Jireh Swift School on Acushnet Avenue near Lund's corner being one of the schools. One of my aunts lives in the area."

O'Malley was forming the opinion, "We are on the right trail. We need to find this man and quickly. If he was in the vehicle that slowed down in front of the State Street house, where was he coming from at this hour of the night?"

Into the Dark

Chapter Twenty-two

The man was driving his van slowly down the street and was again annoyed with the lack of success in his search. He was distracted with his frustration and was just about to turn into the driveway when he saw lights moving in the upstairs room. He straightened the wheels of the vehicle and continued on. He drove away.

Not that long ago he would have immediately called the police. Someone had broken into the house. But he had a secret that would make such an encounter complicated.

He wondered, "How did they enter the house? The front and back doors are securely locked." A few months before he had installed additional sliding bolts. This type of labor was not familiar to him but he was quite pleased with his work. He had followed the instructions carefully. With the assistance of the owner at the hardware store on Purchase Street, he had even procured a small hand drill so that he might fasten the screws securely into the door-jamb.

He was hoping the house wasn't being further vandalized. There wasn't much in the house worth stealing. Over the years practically all of the furnishings had been sold. He had needed additional funds.

He pulled into the parking lot across the street belonging to a nearby church. It was empty at this hour. He needed to rest from his long exasperating day. He needed to think. "What can I do next?" he thought to himself. "Maybe once it's daylight I can go back to the house. Vandals don't usually hang around."

One thought especially infuriated him, "Did they discover my room? Those few possessions are extremely important to me. I don't have the money to replace those suits. And what will I wear to go to work tomorrow?"

He slid down into the seat of the van and closed his eyes. He dozed off and on, constantly being awakened by his anxiety and concerns. "If only things had turned out differently," he pondered.

When the sun rose under the clouds, its warmth entered through the windshield that faced to the east. In this brief feeling of comfort, the man fell into a deep sleep.

Cars driving into the parking lot awakened him. People were gathering for the early Sunday morning ritual. He decided, "I'll go to church." As a child he and his younger brother had attended church quite frequently with his mother. His father, who rose early six days a week, slept in on Sunday mornings.

His father was a conductor on the train that left New Bedford for Boston. The man suddenly recalled the black cap and uniform he wore to work. He had loved to put on his father's cap that slipped over his ears. His brother would laugh at him. Those were happy days.

The man recalled the constant coughing and spitting up that his mother began to exhibit after he had started school. One day when he and his brother returned from school, they had found her laying on the floor. She moved slightly as the two boys tried to help her. Some blood had poured from her mouth and onto her lips. The carpet beneath her was stained.

The man had immediately considered going to one of the neighbors for help but reconsidered. His father and mother were very private people. No one knew of the difficulties his family was experiencing. He had overheard many times his father berating his mother that the house she had inherited from her parents was too large and expensive to keep up on his salary. Now that she was sick, it had taken all she had to keep up the appearance of a genteel household.

The man and his brother helped their mother to the couch. He put a cushion under her head where she was laying and asked his brother to fetch a glass of water. Their mother just lay there. He propped the pillow further up behind her head and tried to bring the glass to her lips. He managed to get a few sips into his mother's mouth but most slipped onto her chin and neck. He remembered how he and his brother cried and just sat there watching over her until their father came home from work.

A few weeks later their mother was diagnosed with tuberculosis and sent to a sanitarium in the far north end of the city. The family doctor had convinced the father that it was necessary to keep their mother separate from the family lest they get infected as well. She would receive ample nutrition, clean air and plenty of rest. There was evidence that such treatment assisted the patients to recover as their own immune systems strengthened.

The day his mother moved to the sanitarium - *the boy* became *the man*. His father initially tried to get a change in his schedule so that he could be home to assist his boys off to school. He had little seniority in the Carmen's Union so he was forced to get up even earlier to prepare something for his boys' breakfast. It was the man's task to see that he and his brother had their breakfast, got dressed for school and got there on time. In the beginning his younger brother had cooperated, but as the time went by he became obstinate and difficult.

The boys' father tried to get some help, especially that first summer once school was let out. His wife had no family. She had been an only child. In his own case, the father had been disowned by his family when he married into the Piedmont family. The family believed he had turned away from his heritage.

The father's parents lived in Brockton. Early in their married life, his mother had invited her son, his wife and young son to the Perruzi home for Christmas. It was a disaster. The words that the father and son had spoken and shouted over dinner had precipitated an early exit with his wife and son, leaving his mother and two sisters in tears. As they walked down the walk to the family car, Mr. Perruzi had bellowed out, "Don't come back!" So they never did.

Into the Dark

Chapter Twenty-three

Inspector O'Malley decided on a plan. Reluctantly, he again called the Police Chief Luke Guerney. He needed authorization to initiate his idea and he needed to do it now.

The Chief answered the telephone on the first ring. Unable to fall back to sleep after O'Malley's initial call, he had quietly washed and dressed. He was drinking a cup of hot coffee sitting at the kitchen table getting ready to go to central headquarters. As a member of the police departments in Springfield and New Bedford, he had come across some very despicable acts that citizens perpetrated on each other out of anger, greed, intoxication and mental instability. Acts against young innocent children were the ones that bothered him the most.

O'Malley brought the Chief up to date on the case. He asked, "Would you authorize me to send out an APB? The bulletin would seek to stop any dark colored van found travelling our local streets. Unfortunately, we don't have a license plate number. It wasn't included in the original file. The Department of Motor Vehicle won't be opened until tomorrow morning. For the sake of this little boy, we can't wait that long."

Police Chief Guerney readily agreed and added, "I'm on my way into headquarters. I'll extend the all-points bulletin to include our neighboring cities and towns. I will also put in a call to the State Police. Having seen that his safe space has been located, he may be on the run."

The sergeant at the front desk prepared and sent out the initial APB to the local police precincts. It included the instructions to bring in for questioning any white male associated with a dark van.

O'Malley wondered whether Charles of different last names might make an appearance at the rooming house. Another part of his plan was to solicit the assistance of Mrs. Laura Nunes. He decided to walk there. It was only a few blocks away from headquarters on Union Street. He needed to instruct Mrs. Nunes carefully about the police interest in her occasional lodger. He also needed to get her to agree to notify the police without telling the lodger of the Inspector's plan to bring him in for questioning. He had sensed on his first visit that Mrs. Nunes policed her own turf.

It was still sometime before day break. Along the way from the police station, O'Malley kept an eye out for a possible dark van parked in the vicinity. He remembered Mrs. Nunes mentioning that Charles Perruzi walking to the lodging house seeking a room. There had been no mention of a vehicle.

Mrs. Nunes answered the rear door dressed with large curlers in her hair covered by some netting. Her disposition hadn't changed. "What do you want now?" was her opening remark.

"Could we talk a bit? It's important. It won't take long," said the Inspector.

Mrs. Nunes opened the door and said, "OK. Come on in."

She brought him into the kitchen. She pointed to a chair at the kitchen table and said, "Have a seat. After you left earlier I couldn't fall back asleep. I decided to make some muffins for my lodgers for part of their Sunday morning breakfast. I was just having a cup of coffee before getting started. Do you want a cup?"

O'Malley agreed, "That would be nice. It's been a long night."

Mrs. Nunes gave the Inspector a mug and pointed, "There's some milk and sugar near the fridge. I can't afford to provide cream like the rich folks."

O'Malley decided to engage her in the hope of thawing the atmosphere, "I used to drink it black, but the stomach isn't like it used to be. I'll get myself some milk. Thank you."

Having filled up her cup and adding two spoons of sugar, she sat down at one of the other kitchen chairs and asked, "So what do you have to say?"

Hoping that the sugar might sweeten her disposition, O'Malley started, "As you know from our earlier visit we have an interest in your sporadic boarder, Mr. Charles Perruzi. We need your help."

Mrs. Nunes answered, "I usually manage my own affairs without the help of the police. I lay down the rules very clearly to my lodgers. They only get one chance and they're out of here. I respect them. I don't meddle in their affairs. As to Mr. Perruzi I have already told you all I know about him."

"We know that," said O'Malley. "However, there may be a chance that he might be looking for a place to stay. We know he comes here on occasion. We would like to question him. If he appeared on the scene in the next few days, would you let us know without informing him of our interest in him? We don't want to scare him off."

Mrs. Nunes considered this for a spell and finally said, "That's not the way I work with my boarders. There would have to be a very good reason for me to change my approach. So far, except for your early hours and persistence indicating something of a serious nature, I don't see any reason to change my way of doing things."

"I respect that," answered O'Malley. "The most that I can reveal to you at his time is that our interest in Mr. Perruzi centers on a missing child."

For the first time, Mrs. Nunes harsh exterior began to ease. "OK. If he shows up, I'll give you a call. The room he used last month is still available."

O'Malley gave her his card. "Please call this number. If I'm not in, someone at the station will answer and know how to locate me. Just mention your name. Thank you for your understanding." Then pointing to his empty cup, he said," You make a good cup of coffee."

O'Malley thought he recognized a tiny smile on Mrs. Nunes face as they rose from the table and she escorted him to the door.

"It's starting to get light out," she said and added with some frustration, "and I haven't started my muffins yet."

Into the Dark

Chapter Twenty-four

Charles joined the early morning Sunday service. His mother had brought him to a Methodist church. They had never been officially registered as parishioners. The pastor would recognize them and was always welcoming even if their attendance was sporadic and infrequent. His younger brother enjoyed the singing but was restless during the time of preaching. Charles always listened attentively. He had an inquisitive mind.

Charles wasn't sure as to the denomination of this particular church. He easily recognized that it was Christian and probably Catholic. He had come to the service seeking solace and some respite. The preaching didn't do anything for him. The words seemed empty especially when a call for service to others focused on money. However, the moments of quiet helped him to overcome his agitation.

For nearly two years now, Charles had volunteered his services to the local Salvation Army located downtown on Purchase Street. He had discovered that the organization had arranged shelter for his brother Curtiss during a particularly long cold snap the previous winter. When he volunteered at the Salvation Army, especially during the Christmas season when he spent days and hours ringing the bells at the red kettles, he normally stayed at a rooming house nearby

Curtiss had become a street person. His mother's hospitalization at the sanitarium had been difficult enough for the whole family. But when she died two years later without returning to their home, Curtiss and his father fell into spells of deep depression. Curtiss exhibited more and more anger. He began stealing and terrorizing neighbors and in his early teen age years would stay away from home for days, only to come home filthy and weakened with hunger. His father had turned to drink and died during those terrible teen years. Charles was left to care for both of them.

Only one aunt had reached out to the family. When Aunt Gwendolyn married she had moved from Brockton to the north end section of New Bedford. She and her husband Peter worked in the mills along the Acushnet River. She was the only family member who had visited the Piedmont residence on State Street.

After high school Charles had gone on to become an accountant. His first job was as a junior accountant at the Goodyear in the south end of the city. He worked long tedious hours and was the only one who brought in a steady paycheck. His brother Curtiss initially did some stints on the fishing boats that left from New Bedford. His share of the catch normally went to drink and women. On rare occasions he would come home directly from a fishing trip and drop off a pile of cash to help support the household and then be off to party. If he started partying immediately after a fishing trip, he would come home penniless.

Charles left the parking lot across from the church and decided to see what was happening at his home. As he was about to turn onto State Street, he discovered that the family homestead that was four houses on the right hand side was encircled with police cars. Again he drove on. For over a year now, Charles had provided meager shelter for his brother in the garage. Earlier in the evening he had been searching the streets and building entrances for Curtiss but without success. When he did find him on occasion, he could sometime entice him to come home and find shelter. Not only was Curtiss a street person but there was a warrant out for his arrest. A few months earlier he had walked out of a court bail hearing.

Charles was exhausted. He needed to eat and sleep. He hoped Mrs. Nunes had a room available for him.

Into the Dark

Chapter Twenty-five

Charles Piedmont parked his van in one of the three spaces in the lot behind the Salvation Army building. During his recent years of volunteer services, the Major had invited him to use this parking area rather than leaving his vehicle parked on the street. Very few people came to the center by car, most members and volunteers were more local and either walked or travelled by bus.

Major Thomas Gilbert was a very religious man. He firmly believed and lived the Army's simple mission, "Heart to God and Hand to Man." Everyone was welcomed. The Sunday Holiness Meetings were well attended. The congregation was a mixture of the poor who received assistance and those who volunteered their services. The Salvation Army as an evangelical part of the universal Christian church provided both opportunities to worship and for Christian service.

The Sunday worship had just ended when Charles arrived. The gathering milled about the combination hospitality/storage room. Charles joined them for coffee and the muffins and rolls neighboring restaurants had dropped off after closing on Saturday. He was known by the group and felt at home. Some of his natural reserve began to diminish and he found himself conversing animatedly with them.

Eventually, Charles took Major Gilbert aside and asked if he could meet with him. The Major answered, "When the group breaks up. You can join me in my office."

Charles was very uneasy as he sat in front of the Major. He wasn't sure where to start. The Major was a warm and unassuming person. Finally, he got the courage to say, "I need some help."

"How may I assist you?" asked the Major.

Charles gave him a brief account of the previous evening, especially his discovery that the police had searched his home. "I'm not worried about myself, but for my brother Curtiss. He's out on the streets again. I searched for him last night but without success."

The Major added, "He has come to us for help in the past. Do you think he will make his way here again?"

"Maybe," answered Charles. "But that's not my major concern. There is a warrant out for his arrest. A month ago he was discovered with a pocketbook that belonged to an elderly woman. She had been accosted by, what she described a bum, who stole it from her even though she had wrapped the straps securely around her arm. The woman sustained some injury to her arm."

"The police locked him up at the Ash Street Jail," he continued. "They contacted me after my brother provided them my name as a contact person. He's never been in this type of trouble before. He's been picked up for disorderly behavior and vagrancy but never for theft and injury."

The Major listened attentively and sympathetically which encouraged Charles to continue his tale.

"I went to court with him for his arraignment," added Charles. "While waiting in the hallway for our proceedings, he excused himself under the pretext of going to the rest room and he never returned. I haven't seen him since. I was hoping to find him and convince him to turn himself in."

The Major offered, "Our people can certainly keep an eye out for him. We will alert you if someone locates his whereabouts."

Charles finally admitted, "There's a little more complication that I need to share with you. About a year ago I was picked up by the police for loitering around places where young children gather, schools, parks. Some women had reported my behavior to the police. No criminal offense was uncovered or proven but I was warned not to frequent such places and that I was on their watch list."

"Well, this past Saturday," Charles continued, "I was in the north end of the city about to visit my aunt who lives there. I noticed two young ones, a boy and a girl, going house to house picking up newspapers. I offered to help. I asked them to follow me to my aunt's house. I was sure she would be willing to help them."

Charles added, almost in tears, "They became frightened and ran off. I was so disappointed and angry. What did I do? Why were people judging my good intentions and making me into a monster? Even little kids." "I believe the police are searching for me," admitted Charles. The Major asked, "So you have in the past loitered around schools? Why?"

Charles thought for a while, "My mother was hospitalized in a sanitarium when I was young and I became responsible for my younger brother, Curtiss. When I see young children playing together and running around, I stop and watch them and think of what we both missed in our youth. I've always been too serious. Even worse, I was a failure with my brother."

The Major said, "I've known you as a good and honest man for quite a while now. Your service to our community is admirable. I would be willing to vouch for you."

Into the Dark

Book Six

Into the Dark

Book Six

Chapter Twenty-six

...into the LIGHT

Everything was quiet in the house when Louise woke up and found herself being crowded by her sister. She slipped out of Charlotte's bed and lay down in her own twin bed.

She immediately thought of Andrew. Wondering how he was. She so wanted to see him and hold him even if he was always dirty and squirmy. She hoped he wasn't afraid. She also thought that he must be hungry. He would have eaten bowls of Mémère's American Chop Suey and endless slices of Sunbeam bread loaded with butter.

At the same time Andrew awakened. He was sitting on a dirt floor with his back against the stone wall of a dark enclosure. He pulled the tuque deeper over his ears. He was grateful now that Charlotte had nagged him to bring it with him. His pea coat kept him warm but his left hand was cold. It had slipped out of his pocket while he slept. He was able to slip his right hand into the section between the buttons of his coat. He thought to himself, "This is why Napoleon kept his hand there."

It was very dark. A little bit of light from outside the enclosure could be seen coming in through the cracks. Andrew had been here all day. He hadn't moved. He felt the apple in his coat pocket. He was famished. Trying to keep any noise or sound to a minimum, Andrew bit into the juicy apple. Without stopping he ate the apple down to the core. He spit out a seed and wiped the back of his hand across his mouth. "That was good," he said to himself.

The small light that was left on at night in the living room shined into the girls' bedroom. The bedroom doors were usually kept ajar during this time of year. The only source of heat in the apartment came from the large all-purpose stove/oven in the living area. Louise felt some comfort in the light. Louise tried to visualize Andrew. She could see him in his blue pea coat. His mother had copied the shape and style from the one her Uncle Claude wore so often when he first came home from the war. Mémère Paradis had found a piece of the navy colored heavy woolen material at one of the department stores. It was Andrew's favorite winter coat.

When Andrew first arrived at this **dark** spot, he just sat there on the cold dirt floor. He shivered with cold and fear. He had backed up as far as he could into the enclosure. He listened for any noise or movement. Quite a bit of light, coming in from outside, allowed him to see his surroundings. It was a small area and a few pieces of cardboard were scattered about. For the longest time Andrew had forced himself to be still and quiet. He could hear Sister Pauline, his teacher at St. Joseph's School, encouraging him to sit quietly and listen. She would be proud of him now. He eventually had fallen asleep.

Louise started to cry. She tried to be quiet so as not to awaken her sister. She had a headache but the pain in her chest was awful. She just wanted to hold her brother's hand. They had done so almost every day when they first walked to and from school. Now, of course, she could hardly keep up to him as he ran along and met up with his friends. However, she had always kept a watchful eye on him except earlier today when she turned and ran.

In the darkness Andrew remembered the cardboard strewn about and decided to fetch some of it. It would be softer to sit on and maybe make it a little warmer than the cold dirt flooring. He moved cautiously and quietly within the small area. His hand felt a piece of the packing material. When he started to drag the piece back to his spot, the noise of the cardboard moving along resounded in the small space. Andrew immediately stopped in his tracks. He knelt there quietly and listened for anything. After a long while he arranged the cardboard near the wall and resumed his spot. The cardboard didn't turn out to be as soft as he had imagined, and it was quite damp.

Louise eventually fell back asleep. In her fitful dream, she was reaching her hand out to Andrew. He kept slipping away from her. But one time, he turned around and looked at her in the eye and gave her that famous mischievous smile.

Now that Andrew had moved about, he started to feel a little bolder. He thought, "Maybe I can go up the few stairs nearby and try the door." He would have to be careful. He didn't know whether the strange man was lurking about outside this small enclosure just waiting for him to make a move.

After a long wait, Andrew got the resolve to venture out of the enclosure. He moved a piece of wooden slat and peered out. He really couldn't see much of anything. Again he listened attentively and heard nothing. He crept out and moved to the stairs on his left. He quietly crawled up the stairs and reached the doorway. He thought to himself, "Do I dare try the handle of the door?"

Eventually he stood up to reach the door handle. It was the first time he had stood erect in hours. It made him feel more courageous but also more vulnerable to being seen. He tried the door knob. It turned but the door did not open. It was locked.

Andrew immediately squatted down and, very disheartened, decided to return to his safety spot sitting on the cardboard.

Into the Dark

Chapter Twenty-seven

Al was initially restless as he twisted and turned but gradually settled down. He and his brothers had a plan. This reassured Al who for years always planned the events of the following day before her fell asleep.

Janet had worked assiduously. The face of the man was being imprinted on her mind. The round cheeks, the bald head, the angry expression all unnerved her as she thought of Andrew who might be in his clutches. Sometime after midnight she and Martha had completed ten posters.

A little later Martha retreated to the downstairs tenement. Janet initially thought to skip her bath. The hour was late. But reflecting that she had worked hard helping her mother and now with all the anxiety, she thought a good long soak in a warm tub would helping her to relax and maybe help her fall asleep.

When she slipped into bed near her sleeping Al, he moved slightly and mumbled something.

In his sleep Al could see that someone was in the dark shadows. He bent over and squinted thinking he recognized Andrew's pea coat. He wanted to go further into the dark area but all his efforts and struggles didn't produce any movement forward. He felt trapped. Even his arms wouldn't move. When he tried to holler out, all he could produce was a weak mutter.

Andrew had again fallen asleep. He had pulled up his knees and in that crouched position slipped the bottom of his pea coat over his legs. He was getting colder and uncomfortable. He wished he was home in his warm bed.

Much later Andrew had awakened again from an uncomfortable sleep and found he was hungry. He noticed that the enclosure was a little lighter. He thought to himself, "It must be getting close to morning."

He continued, "Today is Sunday. Everybody will soon be getting ready to go to Church. I'll be missing a chance to be in the procession at today's Mass."

Andrew had started to learn to be an altar boy. Since Christmas he and six other boys in his class were pulled out of their normal classwork twice a week. Sister Mary Stevens was teaching them the Latin responses used during the ceremony. He especially liked the response to the priest's "Dominus vobiscum." He could blare out with confidence, "Et cum spiritu tuo."

Once a week Father Armand Clouture would march these new recruits to the church. He would stand at the altar and go through a quick version of the Mass. Behind him and facing the altar, the altar boys practiced the proper time to stand and kneel. He and all his friends especially liked to be the one chosen to shake the bell chimes for the moments of consecration.

So far they had only practiced and participated in the processions for the Sunday solemn high Mass. After Easter which was only a few weeks away, they would have the opportunity to serve their first Mass.

Andrew was getting restless. He had just about had enough of this being quiet and silent. He hadn't seen or heard the man for long hours now. Maybe it was time to make a move. His earlier foray to the stairway and door hadn't shown that the man was just waiting for Andrew to make a move. Andrew wondered, "Maybe, he's not even around here."

He decided, "It's time to venture out a little further." Approaching daylight would make things a little easier.

Andrew crawled to the other side of the enclosure, moved the slat and slipped through. He remained motionless for a long time. He could see the stairs to his left that had led to the locked door. Suddenly he froze with fright. He thought he heard some noise from the shadows to his right.

After a while when nothing happened, he began to notice that down at the end of a dark alley that it was increasingly getting brighter. "Do I dare to go that route?" Andrew thought to himself. The light at the end of the tunnel seem to be calling him and made him braver.

Andrew began his slow trek to the light, stopping every few seconds to listen carefully for any sound that might spell danger. He kept moving. A little more quickly each time.

A few streaks of the rising sun greeted him at the end of the journey. "Do I dare to run out into the open?" he wondered.

Into the Dark

Chapter Twenty-eight

Al Lepage woke up long before it was time to meet his brothers. He rose quietly and went to the bathroom. After relieving himself, he washed his face splashing cold water especially around his somewhat puffy eyes. After brushing his teeth, shaving and combing his unruly hair, he returned to the bedroom to dress.

Janet opened her eyes and silently got out of her side of the bed. She put on her housecoat that lay on the chair nearby. She came over to Al and kissed him on the cheek. It had become a habit between them over the years to not kiss on the lips in the morning until both had brushed their teeth.

Janet left the room while Al continued to dress. He didn't wear his usual Sunday garb but the clean work clothes that Janet had laid out for him before she had retired for the night.

As Al exited the room, Janet motioned with a finger on her lips, "Be quiet." She closed the door to the girls' bedroom. Looking in she saw that both girls were in their separate twin beds.

Janet said, "I'll make some coffee. We still have a few corn muffins or would you rather have some toast?"

Al answered, "I won't have anything right now. I want to go to communion this morning. Andrew can use all of God's goodness we can muster."

Janet agreed. "Let me show you the posters that Martha and I prepared last night," she said. "We had enough paper to do ten of them." She added with a shudder, "That face haunted me all night."

Al held Janet close to him. "I'll take a couple with us to church. I'm quite sure we'll get permission to place one at the front of the building. Labonte's drug store will be opened after Mass and we'll drop one off there before my brothers and I start searching the neighborhood."

Al tried to go quietly down the back stairway. This was not one of his strong points. He usually announced his arrival long before he arrived at a doorway.

His brother Joseph was ready and waiting. The rest of the household was quiet. It was a family custom to attend the 8 o'clock Mass. It was a little after 5:30. Pierre told Al, "Claude said he would meet us on the sidewalk."

Sure enough Claude was waiting for them. The three brothers jumped into Al's truck and off they drove the few blocks to the church. They entered the side door to St. Joseph's Church. Al broke off from the group and with a poster in hand went to the sacristy to see the priest who was to say the Mass. He found the young newly assigned curate putting on his vestments.

The word had been around the neighborhood and Father Richard Renaud was aware that Andrew had gone missing. Al said, "We haven't found Andrew. We prepared some posters and wondered if we could place one at the front entrance of the church. My wife, Janet, drew this sketch of the man suspected of taking Andrew. My daughter, Louise, who was with Andrew gave us this description. We hope that someone may recognize him and he may be apprehended before something terrible happens to…Andrew."

Father Renaud tried to reassure Al, "I'll mention about Andrew and will ask the parishioners to offer any assistance, especially their prayers. We have to have hope. After Mass I'll speak with the Monsignor about the poster. I don't think he will object but I don't want to overstep my bounds."

Al left a poster in the sacristy. He entered the nave of the church by the side entrance and found his two brothers in the front pew. Their comfort level was normally to the rear of the congregation but today was different. Within a few minutes the bell attached to the sacristy door rang to announce the entrance of the priest and two altar boys.

With his back to the small gathering for the early morning Mass, Father Renaud stepped up to the altar and began the prayers of the Eucharistic celebration. The altar boys knelt behind him. The one to the right was a bit of a fidget. Al recognized him as one of the cousins who lived next door.

After his sermon which Father Renaud read from the pulpit, he told them briefly of Andrew's plight. He kept the details to a minimum. He asked for prayers and said that the Lepage family would appreciate any assistance in finding their young boy.

After Mass the Lepage brothers drove to Labonte's Pharmacy. Sarah Labonte was setting up the counter for the early morning trade, mostly people who had just left the church nearby. Some were already sitting at the counter waiting for their morning cup of coffee. Others kept filing into the shop and picking up a copy of one of the Boston papers that had been dropped off earlier at the drug store's entrance and were now stacked inside. Most just dropped a quarter on the counter and were off.

Those who had just attended Mass questioned the Lepage brothers. "When did this happen?" asked one.

Joseph answered, "Yesterday afternoon."

There was mumbling among the patrons at the counter. They were filling in on the details and rumors that were going through the neighborhood.

Al produced the poster and asked Sarah if he could leave one with her. She readily agreed.

Al asked the people at the counter, "Do any of you recognize this man?

Only one said, "There some resemblance to a man who lives above the Avenue on Princeton Street."

"Do you know his name?" asked an encouraged Al.

"No," he answered. "But he lives just a few houses away from my in-laws. "There address is 327. They live on the second floor. They should be able to tell you his name and his exact address. I can go with you, if you want."

Al readily agreed. Claude and Joseph decided to start their door to door combing of the neighborhood.

The man jumped into Al's truck and introduced himself as Peter Marien, "I live a few blocks north of Brooklawn Park. It's a single family. My wife and I just bought the house. I remember you delivering milk to the family home when I was a kid. You must be a wreck."

As they drove up Princeton Street, he said, "My in-laws' house is on the right hand side. From all his days delivering house to house Al was familiar with the pattern of addresses in the city. For streets going east and west crossing the major avenues, the even numbers were all on the south side of the street.

Al suggested, "I'll wait down here. It's still early and they may need some time before they are ready for visitors. If they want to see me, just come and get me." He gave Peter a poster.

A few minutes later Peter was at the front door waving Al to come and as they went up the stairs to the second floor said, "They don't think it resembles the man I thought was one of their neighbors."

Peter's in-laws were still scrutinizing the poster as the two men entered the apartment. Peter's father-in-law said, "This rendering is too young looking. Our neighbor, Clifford Baker is quite elderly. He is bald with straggly hair around his ears and has a similar round face. However, he uses a cane and seldom ventures too far without assistance."

Al was disappointed at this revelation. Louise's description of the man and his movements could not fit a man who had difficulty walking.

Al dropped off Peter at the drug store. Peter embarrassingly stated, "I'm sorry it didn't work out."

Al answered, "It was a lead. We'll just keep looking."

Into the Dark

Chapter Twenty-nine

Andrew finally got up some courage. He looked out both sides of the alley. Everything was quiet. He was only a short distance from a front gate. He would have to expose himself as he crossed from the alley and over the grass in front of the house to reach the gate.

Making a swift sign of the cross, Andrew darted out into the open and dashed to the gate. There he waited and looked around. The familiar house behind him was all quiet. Only a light in the first floor hallway was on. All the apartments were dark.

It was getting brighter but the earlier sun rays he had seen were now behind heavy clouds. A wet mist was coming from the Acushnet River just behind the many mills that bounded it.

Andrew knew he couldn't just stay there. He had to open the gate and venture out. He stood up and with some effort was able to open the latch. The gate squeaked as he opened it. He slipped out.

He was on the sidewalk. Safety was just across the street. A few houses on the opposite side of the street had lights on. People were up.

There were a few cars parked along the street.

Again taking a deep breath, he got up his courage and ran across the street.

Andrew was now in familiar territory. He raced up the sidewalk. He passed his cousins' house and finally reached the well-known driveway. He had expected to see his father's truck parked there. It wasn't.

He ran to the back door and out of breath finally opened it. He was safe.

He entered the hallway and went directly to the first floor apartment. When he opened the door, he saw his Pépère sitting there reading the Sunday newspaper. Pépère who was always quiet and hardly ever raised his voice, looked up and actually shrieked, "Is that you, Andrew?"

Andrew almost collapsed with relief. He was home.

The unusual outburst from Pépère brought the women in the house out of their rooms where they were preparing themselves for Mass.

His aunt Clara was the first one to reach Andrew. She grabbed him and held him. "Where have you been? Are you alright?"

Mémère joined them and also inquired, "What happened? How did you get here?"

Aunt Martha held back and said, "Give him some room to breathe. He needs time to answer our questions."

Mémère took off his tuque that was still pulled down over his ears. "You're frozen," she exclaimed. "You poor thing. Come here near the stove and get warm."

Into the Dark

Book Seven

Into the Dark

Book Seven

Chapter Thirty

Coming together …

The early morning sun that had been shining under the clouds was now hidden by the dark, heavy clouds. The cold mist threatened to turn to rain. People were heading out to church with heavy rain coats and umbrellas.

Detective Paul Griffin returned to the police station around 8 o'clock. He had alerted Inspector O'Malley that the search had produced some helpful information in the search for the man with the van.

Paul Griffin started, "Someone has been living in the garage. The person living in the house must have helped and fed that person. The area of the garage and mattress were filthy and smelled of cheap whiskey. Plates from the kitchen of the house were discovered in the garage."

O'Malley inquired, "Were you able to discover anything that might assist us in locating Charles Piedmont? It seems we scared him off. It frightens me to think what might happen to the young Lepage boy if our suspect panics."

Paul answered, "We did find evidence that Charles Piedmont worked at the Goodyear. Among his few belongings was a badge that listed him as a Junior Accountant for the factory. We may be able to find something there that may assist us. Even on a Sunday morning, we should be able to locate someone at the plant to help us."

"What's the status at the State Street residence?" asked O'Malley.

Paul answered, "I sent Gus and Bill home and left only one policeman to watch the house in the event someone might turn up. He's observing the house from an unmarked car."

Inspector O'Malley informed Paul Griffin, "We put out an ABP on the van."

"I know," answered Paul. "A squad car brought us the word."

O'Malley continued, "I also revisited Mrs. Nunes at her rooming house and she reluctantly agreed to inform us if Charles Perruzi seeks shelter there. She's a no nonsense person and is very supportive of her lodgers as long as they follow her house rules. She's not inquisitive about their personal lives and avoids interfering in their life outside the house. She only agreed to contact us if he returns to the rooming house when I mentioned that the disappearance of a youngster was part of our investigation."

O'Malley suggested, "Why don't you go home? Get something to eat and clean up and then pursue your lead at the Goodyear."

Paul Griffin agreed and picking up his portable radio said, "It seems like forever since we were listening to the Celtics."

"Keep in touch," advised O'Malley. "I'm also going home to freshen up. Then I'm going to go visit the Lepages and see if there are any developments there."

Into the Dark

Chapter Thirty-one

While Inspector O'Malley was cleaning up at his home, changing his under shirt after washing under his sweaty arm pits, Mary came to the bathroom door and told him, "There's a call for you."

He went downstairs and said, "This is Inspector O'Malley."

The person on the other end said, "We just got a call from the north end precinct. They asked us to alert you that there have been some unexpected developments at the Lepages."

O'Malley replied, "Tell them I will be there shortly."

Mary was ironing a fresh shirt for her husband. "Here take this," she said as he was making his way back to the bathroom.

She continued, "You should eat. Do you want me to make you some eggs and toasts?"

"OK," answered O'Malley, "but no coffee. I'll have a glass of milk."

O'Malley's daughters were starting to awaken for their Sunday attendance at the 10 o'clock Mass. When they came down to the kitchen and found their father all dressed and having a quick breakfast, they were disappointed to discover that he was on his way out again. They worried about him. The glass of milk was an evident clue that their father wasn't feeling well.

When Inspector O'Malley arrived at the Lepage's home, many neighbors were milling around on the sidewalk. One could recognize the relief on their faces as they spoke animatedly with each other. Under their winter coats O'Malley noticed all forms of half-dressed attire.

Officer Matt Cyr was back on duty and met with O'Malley near the unmarked police car. "I have few details," he started. "About an hour ago young Andrew Lepage walked into his grandparents' tenement. His father and two uncles who were scouring the neighborhood just came back from their search. It was the neighbors who told them that the young boy they were searching for was home. Words spreads fast in this type of a close neighborhood."

The Inspector inquired, "Have you seen the young boy? What shape is he in?"

Officer Cyr said, "No. I haven't seen him. There was too much activity and excitement going on in that household. I thought it was best to give them some private time and wait for your arrival. Those milling about are saying that he is well except for being cold and hungry."

A wave of chaotic joy greeted O'Malley. The entire family was gathered around young Andrew. His sister Louise was holding on to him and not about to let him go.

O'Malley spotted Martha and recognizing his inquiring eyes, she came over to him.

The Inspector asked her, "Has Andrew been able to tell the family what happened to him?"

Martha answered, "Not really. There's so much excitement at his return and so much kissing that the poor boy hasn't had a moment to say anything."

O'Malley asked, "Do you think we can find a quiet place so that you may help me get him to relate what happened to him?"

Martha responded, "We could go up to his family's apartment on the third floor."

O'Malley glanced around the room and suggested, "We should have his sister Louise accompany him. On second thought I think his parents and his other sister should be with us too. Even though he looks so brave right now, I think he needs all his natural support around him to relive these past hours with us."

"I agree," said Martha. "If anyone wasn't present, they would feel terribly anxious and rejected. I'll try to manage his story so that any despicable incidents are not too descriptive so as not to alarm and frighten his sisters."

"Thank you," answered O'Malley.

Martha said, "Leave it to me to gather the clan." Sure enough in a few minutes later the gathering parted and the Al Lepage family were on their way to their apartment."

Martha accompanied by Janet led Andrew and his sisters upstairs. O'Malley and Al trailed behind them.

Al still had a look of anguish on his face. He panted out the words, "I had a nightmare last night where I was reaching to Andrew but couldn't extend my arms out to him. Now he's home. Somehow I feel this has all been a bad dream."

On the second landing, O'Malley put a supportive hand on Al's shoulder. O'Malley said, "It's real Al. Andrew is home with you and the family. He is safe."

O'Malley continued, "We need to find out what happened. We have some leads as to the man in question. I'm hoping that Andrew can provide additional clues so that we may apprehend him."

Martha arranged the seating arrangement with Andrew between his sisters and their mother Janet on the couch. In the meantime, O'Malley spotted a copy of the poster that Janet had made up the previous evening.

Al told him, "We started to place the posters around the neighborhood. There's one at the church, one at the drug store and we were showing it to the neighbors when we got word that Andrew was home."

Martha placed a chair for Al near Janet and two dining room chairs facing them. Again O'Malley chair was slightly behind Martha's, she would bring a less threatening atmosphere to the interview.

Martha started, "Andrew, we are so happy to have you home with us. You have no idea."

Tears flowed gently down all the faces of those on the couch, except for Andrew. Martha wondered, "He may still be in shock. I need to proceed cautiously."

She added, "Your sister, Louise is a very brave girl. She told us what happened before you disappeared. She was very disappointed in herself for leaving you behind. I don't think she's ever going to let go of your hand."

Andrew and Louise just looked at each other. Andrew slipped his hand out of hers and gave his sister a huge hug.

"Now, Andrew can you tell us what happened since Louise last saw you," asked his Aunt Martha.

Andrew thought for a while, and proudly said, "Ma tante, I ran away and found one of my hiding places."

Martha sought more information, "When and how did you run away?"

Andrew holding on to his sister's hand answered, "I heard Louise calling me to turn around and to run home. I was on the path in the corner lot and when I went to turn my wagon it got stuck in the bushes. I pulled and pulled. I was afraid the man would turn around and come after me. So I left my wagon stuck in the path and ran."

Andrew continued, "When I reached the sidewalk, I looked back. The man was coming after me. My wagon blocked the path. While he was picking it up and throwing it into the bushes. I ran across the street and hid behind a car parked in a driveway. After a while I sneaked behind the house where Mon Oncle Claude and Ma Tante live. During the summer time," he said looking to his mother, "you would bring me over to their backyard where Ma Tante Anne would read to me. One day I discovered a good hiding place under the back porch. There was a loose board. That's where I was hiding all night."

Martha guardedly asked, "Did the man find you?"

"No," answered Andrew.

A sigh of relief escaped from all the adults in the room. The worst nightmares that each had foreseen had not been realized. Al closed his eyes and abruptly embraced Janet.

"So you stayed there all night?" inquired Martha.

"That's right," answered Andrew. "Once during the night I came out of the hiding place and tried the back door on the porch, but it was locked. I was afraid he might still be looking for me, so I went back quickly to my spot. This morning when the sun came up, I felt brave and decided to run home."

"So you never saw the man after you ran across the street, correct?" asked Martha.

"That's right," answered Andrew.

Martha continued, "Your sister Louise gave us a description of the man and your mother drew a picture." Picking up the poster, she asked, "Does this look like him?"

"I guess so," answered Andrew. "I never really looked at him. He was scary."

O'Malley sensed that Andrew was ready to move on from this episode in his young life, and said, "You're a brave young man, Andrew. You showed lots of courage and cunning in your escape. You're now home safe and sound. We are all so relieved."

Into the Dark

Chapter Thirty-two

When Inspector Daniel O'Malley returned to his office at the downtown police station, he went immediately to the Chief's office.

Chief Luke Guerney had already been informed that the young boy had been found. O'Malley brought him up-to-date. "From what Andrew Lepage told us the man in question did not even touch him. Andrew ran away and hid himself in one of the neighboring backyards across the street. Our searches of the neighborhood earlier in the evening had concentrated on the side of the street where he lived."

Chief Guerney looked at a very weary Inspector and said, "Now that we know the boy is safe, the pressure of time in this case has been lifted. I want you to go home, get some rest and we'll start fresh Monday morning."

O'Malley thanked him and added, "Detective Paul Griffin is conducting an investigation at the Goodyear plant today. He should be sent home when he completes that inquiry. He's also been up all night."

The Chief told O'Malley, "I'll see what he turns up at the Goodyear. He's much younger than you and I'm sure he's gone without sleep on more than one occasion. He was quite a party person in the days when he was still on patrol."

Before leaving, O'Malley tried to synopsize the case with the Chief, "We have someone watching the State Street residence in the event Charles, whatever his last name is, returns there. Mrs. Nunes has agreed to inform us if he returns to the boarding house."

Chief Guerney added, "We have put out an APB for the vehicle in the city and neighboring towns."

"Oh," remembered O'Malley, "I have a poster in my car that Andrew's mother drew up last night. It has a sketch of our suspect. I threw it into the back seat and forgot to bring it in. I'll get it. There are a few posted out there in the north end neighborhood."

The Chief tried to reassure O'Malley, "This case will be my top priority today. So just go home and get some well-deserved rest."

"Also," continued O'Malley, "when the Registry of Motor Vehicle opens tomorrow we should be able to get the license plate number. We also have the name of the cleaners where Charles had his shirts pressed. They'll be open on Monday."

"That's what I'm trying to tell you, O'Malley. There will be plenty to do on Monday," insisted Chief Guerney. "I can coordinate things here until Monday. I have some resources at my disposal. Now go."

O'Malley left the Chief's office. A few minutes later, he came rushing back with the poster. "This should be helpful."

The Chief looked at it closely and then returning a glare to O'Malley, said, "Go!"

When O'Malley arrived at home, his wife and girls were gone to church. He went upstairs and took a warm shower. A year earlier they had installed one of these encircling bars above the tub that held a curtain to hold the spray from wetting the walls and floor of the bathroom. A pipe led from the faucet bringing both cold and hot water to a round device with multiple holes in it, similar to those used on watering cans for the garden."

He put on his long-legged pajamas and a robe and returned to the lower floor. The aroma that came from Mary's kitchen lured a hungry and weary man. He took the lid off the pot on the stove and discovered that Mary was preparing her famous pot roast for the family's Sunday dinner. To the usual potatoes, carrots and onions, Mary added fresh beets which gave the roast a distinctive color and flavor.

Daniel O'Malley took one of the biscuits that Mary had already baked to go with dinner. He smiled. His wife knew that he especially enjoyed dipping a piece of her biscuits into the juices of the roast.

With a glass of milk, he went into the front room and sat in his chair. He put his feet up on the settee and before finishing his biscuit and milk was fast asleep.

That's where his wife and daughters found him. Mary hushed her excited Julia, half way through her, "Daddy's home..."

"Let your father rest," she said. "Let's go about our day but quietly. I'll keep an eye on him and will send him up to our bed, when he begins to stir. We'll all have dinner together when he gets up."

Both girls went to their rooms. Margaret hung up her Sunday clothes, straightened out her room and went back to her books. Julia threw off her clothes on her bed and put on what people called tights. At Julia's insistence Julia's mother had made her tights from a pink colored material. The other girls at the ballet school wore the traditional dark colored material. Julia just loved to be flashy and noticed. She started practicing her steps and routines.

While working in the kitchen, Mary began hearing some movement in the front room. Danny had awakened unsure as to where he was. Mary had earlier closed the curtains in the room. It was darkened and a steady rain was hitting the windows.

Mary encouraged, "Let's get you up to bed. We'll all have dinner together later."

The girls heard some commotion on the stairway and exited their room to see their mom signaling them to be quiet as she led Danny into the room and off to bed. Danny started to awaken and was about to enter his usual routine with Mary whenever he returned home. He would share the events of the day, of course not the details of a case. Then he wanted to hear all that had happened with the family.

Mary said, "Just get to bed now and sleep. Later we will all get together and share our day."

With little reluctance, Danny complied. After checking with her girls, Mary found that her Danny was already breathing heavily and fast asleep. She was grateful.

Into the Dark

Chapter Thirty-three

Early Monday morning Inspector O'Malley sat at his desk reviewing the reports of the previous day. He was well rested and his sharp mind was ready to continue on the case of Andrew Lepage.

There were no developments at the State Street residence nor at the boarding house. Detective Paul Griffin had confirmed that a Charles Piedmont did in fact work as an accountant at the Goodyear plant. The plant opened early each morning but the accounting department's hours were normally 9 to 5.

Charles Piedmont was respected for his work but hardly socialized with others. Chief Luke Guerney had left instructions to have two police officers in the vicinity of the accounting office at the plant by 8. Their instructions were to bring in Charles Piedmont for questioning.

While looking over this material, the energetic young man, Detective Paul Griffin came tumbling into the room. He had also been sent home by the Chief. The team was fit and ready for action.

The time was approaching 7 a.m. O'Malley instructed Detective Griffin to join the two police officers at the Goodyear plant, "Tell the uniformed police officers to keep a low profile and out of sight. I don't want to spook him. He's already aware of some disruption at his home on State Street. He hasn't to date taken up residence at Mrs. Nunes lodging house. He may be in hiding already. But I suspect he is a man of routine and would find it difficult not to go to his normal place of employment."

Paul Griffin agreed, "I learned that Mr. Piedmont has been employed at the Goodyear for over ten years and he's never missed a day of work in all that time."

By 8 o'clock Detective Griffin had spoken with the day manager of the plant about the plan to bring one of their employees in for questioning. He situated himself in a small waiting area outside the accounting office located in a small building attached to the main plant. The small administration building offered some respite from the mechanical noises emanating from the production of tires. The New Bedford plant was producing a new line of nylon threaded tire.

At precisely 8:45 a.m. Charles Piedmont drove into the parking lot of the Goodyear. He found a quiet spot behind the main plant. Some in the administration building had designated places to park near that structure. Even as chief accountant and assistant to the comptroller, Charles had never requested a parking spot nor had one been offered to him.

Charles opened his umbrella upon closing the door to his van. The rain had continued throughout the night. As he approached the administration building he noticed a police vehicle parked nearby. He stopped in his tracks. He wondered, "Have the police found some evidence as to where I work?"

He made a very difficult decision. "I can't go in there right now. I may lose my job. But I need to put some things in order before I meet again with the police." He remembered his last interview with them.

He decided to return to the Salvation Army offices and seek some help.

Into the Dark

Book Eight

Into the Dark

Book Eight

Chapter Thirty-four

Unraveling identities ...

By 9:30 a.m. Detective Paul Griffin approached one of the secretaries in the administration office, and asked, "Did Mr. Charles Piedmont show up for work this morning? Could he have entered this building by another entrance?"

A pretty petite young woman with dark hair and bright red lipstick, answered, "I'll check in the accounting office. He didn't come by my desk."

As she proceeded to a door at the rear of the office, Paul Griffin's eyes were attracted to the shapely derriere that swished and swayed. He looked to see if there was any placard on her desk with her name on it. He couldn't see one. He had become distracted and thought to himself, "I might like to spend some time with that beauty."

Paul's reverie was interrupted by her return. She said, "No, Mr. Charles Piedmont did not show up for work this morning. He didn't call in with an excuse either or that he may be late. The comptroller told me that Mr. Piedmont has never missed a day of work during his entire tenure at the company."

Paul had to try to concentrate on what she was telling him. Her reappearance in the office and approach to her desk was equally appealing as her earlier departure. His eyes focused on her breasts and he found himself straining to lift them to focus on very seductive lips.

Paul took out his note pad, and asked, "Could I have your name and telephone number? We may need to contact you later in this investigation."

Now sitting behind her desk, she said, "I'm Gloria Cordeiro. You can reach me through the main switchboard of the company. The operator will transfer the call. Would it be helpful to have my home number?"

Paul couldn't believe it. He sensed a little chemistry going on between them. Gulping a bit, he answered, "Yes, that certainly would be helpful." He wrote down her home number in his pad.

As he left the building, he tore out the sheet with the number from his pad and placed it in his vest pocket. This would not be part of his report.

By 10 o'clock Detective Griffin was relating the failed attempt to locate Charles Piedmont at his place of employment at the Goodyear. "I left one police officer on site in the event he may show up later."

Paul Griffin was experiencing a jumble of emotions. Professionally, he had been elated with the discovery of Charles' place of employment and had expected to unravel the case by bringing him in for questioning. He was disappointed that Charles had slipped through the noose. Personally, he was aroused by his meeting with Gloria. Plans were already taking shape in his mind as to how to get her to go out with him.

In the meantime, Inspector O'Malley brought his attention back to the case. "We were able to get the license registration for the vehicle. This information has been added to the APB. However, since he hasn't returned to his home and didn't show up for work this morning, I'm wondering if he hasn't left the area under the cover of darkness early Sunday morning."

"Paul, I want you to go to the Bristol County Registry of Deeds office. Search the title for the house on State Street. Get a good history of its owners. Go to the city's assessors and tax offices and do a similar search. We need to uncover a lot more about this family and the strange picture we have of a Charles Piedmont, who at times presents himself as Charles Perruzi."

Into the Dark

Chapter Thirty-five

Detective Paul Griffin spent a few hours researching records at the Registry of Deeds on 6th Street and then the city hall nearby. He had uncovered some interesting history and facts that would be helpful in the investigation.

A steady and cold rain had started about noon. He turned up his collar of his trench coat and firmly set his new purchase on his head. He had bought a new dark blue fedora from Harry the Hatter. Mr. Cabral, the owner, had personally assisted in the purchase. He had pointed out the necessity of being aware of one's height, weight and even skin and eye coloring in the selection of a fedora. It helped determine the width of the rim, the color and material of the band, and the size of the sculptured top and front.

Paul wished that he had taken his old hat with him today. It had threatened to rain for the last few days but he couldn't resist the opportunity of showing off his sharp fedora. Now it was getting all wet. He would have to return to see Mr. Cabral and learn the secrets of restoring his hat to its original shape.

After hanging up his wet coat and hat on the rack on the wall of the small office he shared with two other detectives, Paul grabbed his soggy briefcase and proceeded to Inspector O'Malley's office. Along the way he stopped at the rest room and after using the facility, he also took a towel and wiped down his briefcase that held his faithful notepad and other items he had collected on his search. He didn't want to make a mess of his boss's desk and office.

O'Malley greeted him "What were you able to find out?"

"First," answered Paul, "The Piedmont residence was built in 1855. It's listed as a Greek Revival structure but the assistant at the Registry was quick to point out to me that it is only a "vernacular interpretation". That's a quote. It was purchased from a Thomas Crawford. He was the builder of many of these larger estates as well as modest single-family dwellings that are scattered throughout Acushnet Heights."

Looking through his notes Paul Griffin continued, "The assistant, an elderly Mrs. Colby, who just seems to love these old record books, revealed that buildings in the district were built of uniform scale, with no buildings being higher than four stories. The neighborhood went through a transformation with the construction of the Wamsutta Mills just below the heights. The Wamsutta developed a worker housing development among these fine estates and single family homes. Worker duplexes, two-family tenement homes, triple-deckers and six-family apartment blocks are scattered throughout and were built specifically to accommodate a new wave of immigrants to work in the mills."

Inspector O'Malley appreciated the history lesson, but was also impatient to learn something about the Piedmonts. He asked, "When did the Piedmonts become associated with this property?"

Paul Griffin answered, "Mr. Archibald Piedmont purchased the home from the builder, Thomas Crawford, in 1847. He was an architect with a firm in New York City and was the on-site supervisor during the construction phase of the original Wamsutta mill. Mrs. Colby was proud to inform me that the stone, five story structure was designed by Seth Ingalls of New Bedford."

Paul continued, "Mr. Piedmont stayed on not only for the construction phase but also for the setup of the mill with its 10,000 spindles. The former Congressman Joseph Grinnell from New Bedford, who was one of the major stockholders, was elected the mill's first president. Business began to boom and plans were soon being made to construct a second four story mill. Joseph Grinnell persuaded Archibald Piedmont to take up permanent residence in the city. They would become friends and a great working team. Before Grinnell retired in 1874, Archibald Piedmont had supervised the construction of a fourth even bigger mill."

Inspector O'Malley questioned, "What about Mr. Piedmont's family?"

"I was just getting to that," replied the Detective. "First, the Piedmont name is on the title to this day. Charles and a Curtiss Piedmont are listed on the current title. It was passed on to them from their mother, Angela Piedmont."

Paul Griffin's face suddenly lit up saying, "Here is a piece of information I picked up at the city hall, Angela Piedmont married a James Perruzi."

"That is very enlightening," stated the Inspector. "It explains the name discrepancy."

"Before we focus on this fact," advised the Detective, "let me add some further things I uncovered about the Piedmonts. Archibald died suddenly a few years after the construction of the Mill # 4. His wife Harriet who came originally from New York City decided to return there. Mrs. Colby informed me that the rumor in the day was that Harriet despised the damp, cold and boring New Bedford. She pined for the excitement of the big city, its theater and culture. Her one daughter moved with her to New York and Harriet left the home on State Street to her son, Clyde. His name appears on the land title in 1880."

Detective Paul Griffin continued, "Clyde was quite the dapper in his day. He had married a young woman from Dartmouth. They had only one child, Angela, the mother of our Charles and his

146

brother, Curtiss. Clyde never worked but used his family's wealth to invest in the stock market. He was very successful. He owned one of the first wooden boats, a 1905 Torpedo Stern Launch, that he kept at the affluent coastal village of Padanaram in South Dartmouth. However, as with so many others, the stock market crash in 1920 ruined the Piedmont empire. It's never recovered."

"Clyde and his wife died in a car accident on their way to visit his mother in New York. The accident occurred in Connecticut, near Bridgeport. It happened in 1918. That's when Angela's name appears on the title. A year prior, city records show that Angela married a James Perruzi from Brockton. Angela died of consumption at the Sassaquinn nursing home in 1931. Her sons were young when she died. According to Mrs. Colby, James tried to honor his wife's wishes to keep the homestead but his meager salary made the promise exceedingly difficult. He sold off furnishings and the family retreated to the rear of the building. Interestingly, at their mother's death, the boys inherited the home not their father."

The Inspector was putting all this information together and trying to find some clue as to what direction to go with it. He said, "So Charles has a brother. This is the first we've heard of him. Were you able to discover anything about him?"

"No," answered Griffin. "He's not listed on the voting records of the city. Our search of the home, doesn't give any indication that he lived there."

O'Malley conjectured, "Since his name is still on the title, we can assume that he is alive. Let me ask someone to check our police files and see if there any reference to a Curtiss Piedmont."

As O'Malley picked up the phone to give his instructions, Paul Griffin interrupted, "Let's not forget, Curtiss may be using his father's name - Perruzi."

A few minutes later, the phone on O'Malley desk rang. After writing down some notes, O'Malley informed Griffin, "There's a Curtiss Perruzi in the files with a warrant out for his arrest. He's listed as a vagrant with no known address. The warrant is almost two weeks old. He walked out of a bail hearing."

Into the Dark

Chapter Thirty-six

After making a quick exit from the Goodyear parking lot, Charles Piedmont returned to the Salvation Army. Major Gilbert had allowed Charles to use one of the two small rooms at the rear of their building on Sunday. This was not a normal procedure but under the unusual circumstances, Major Gilbert thought it advisable to offer Charles this accommodation.

Charles Piedmont assured him, "I'll check with the rooming house tomorrow and see if they have room." The Major was aware of these previous arrangements that Charles had used especially during his longer volunteering shifts during the cold Christmas season.

The Major wasn't in the building when he arrived. The place was busy. Volunteers were arranging donated used clothing on racks. Once a week people were invited to come in and pick up clothing for themselves and their family members. If they could afford it, a good number would leave a small donation.

Charles was extremely dejected. Without a job, how could he provide for himself and his brother. He couldn't follow up on his previous plan to rent a room at the boarding house.

Around noon time, the Major knocked on the door of his room. The Major said, "People up front told me that you had returned some time ago. What happened with work?"

Charles answered, "I spotted a police car near the entrance of the administration building and I wasn't ready to be questioned and held – not with my brother still out there."

The Major sat on the bed and invited Charles to sit on the small wooden high back chair in the room. Charles looked inquisitively.

The Major started, "Charles, I have some bad news. I was called to the morgue at St. Luke's Hospital to help identify a body. The police know that I am familiar with many of the street persons of the city."

Charles held his breath and blared out, "Was it Curtiss?"

The Major tearfully nodded. "I'm so sorry Charles. He was found behind one of the mills. They are still trying to determine the cause of your brother's death. They mentioned that there was no evidence of trauma or violence. They surmised that he was there for about two days."

Charles head fell to his lap. He held both knees as he sat, desperately holding back his tears. The Major stood and kneeling before Charles caressed his head trying to comfort him. Finally, a torrent of cries and tears escaped.

After a while, the Major suggested that he would go to the dining room and get them something to eat. "We can have some lunch together right here."

Major Gilbert shared the disturbing news to a few of the regulars. They all felt so awful for their brother, Charles. He was always such a gentle soul, capable and contributed so much to their cause of assisting those in need.

When the Major returned to Charles' room, he found him getting ready to leave. He said, "Thank you but I'm not hungry. I need to go."

"I understand," said the Major. "It's raining very hard out. Be sure to dress properly. You are welcome to look through our clothing racks up front to help protect you from the weather. Be sure to come back when you are ready. This is your home. We'll be waiting for you."

Charles went directly to his van parked behind the building. He drove to the hardware store. He bought a ten-foot length of a larger type hose. Sometime earlier he had purchased one for the house on State Street. The clerk had recommended this type of hose that could attach to a drain pipe and would lead the water away from the building.

In the heavy rain, he drove to the south end of the city. He went to Hazelwood Park. The place was deserted. He backed his van up to an abandoned building. He took the hose and fitted it onto the tail pipe and slipped it through the back doors of the van.

He sat down in the driver's seat and turned on the engine. He could see from the hillside the beach and water that faced the town of Dartmouth. His heart kept crying out, "I'm sorry, Curtiss. I tried…"

Slowly his eyes closed and a darkness enveloped him. Gradually he allowed himself to go …into the **dark**.

ABOUT THE AUTHOR

Clement R. Beaulieu is a semi-retired income tax preparer. In the off-season he wrote and published three historical mystery novels entitled, *Bad Lucky Number*, circa 1930, *Round Corners*, circa 1940, and *Two by Each*, circa 1950, set in the mill city of New Bedford, MA. He lives with his wife, Jo-Ann in the quaint neighboring town of Fairhaven. They have two daughters, Sarah and Julia, who live nearby.

Contact the author at:
Clement R. Beaulieu
346 Sconticut Neck Road
Fairhaven, MA 02719-1318
Phone: 508-993-8659
CLEMCTP@COMCAST.NET